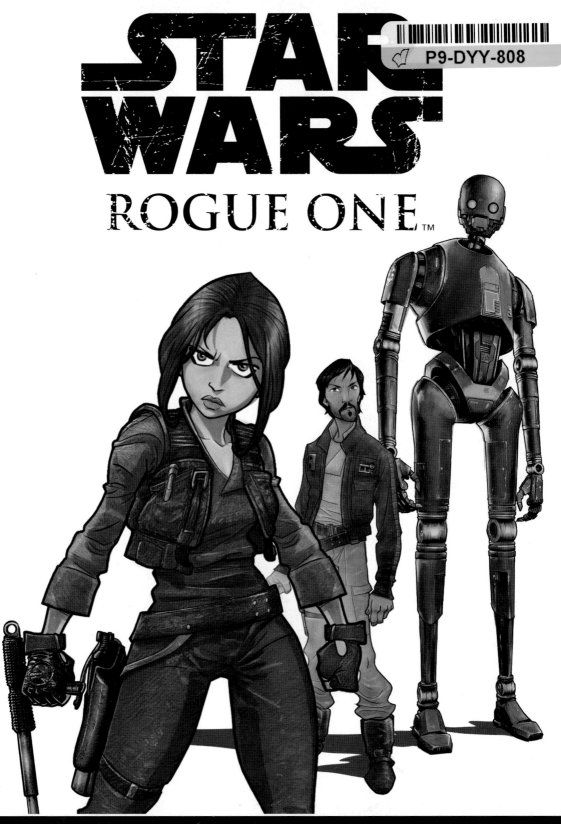

STAR WARS

ROGUE ONE™

A LONG TIME AGO IN A GALAXY FAR, FAR AWAY...

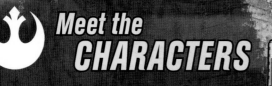

Meet the CHARACTERS

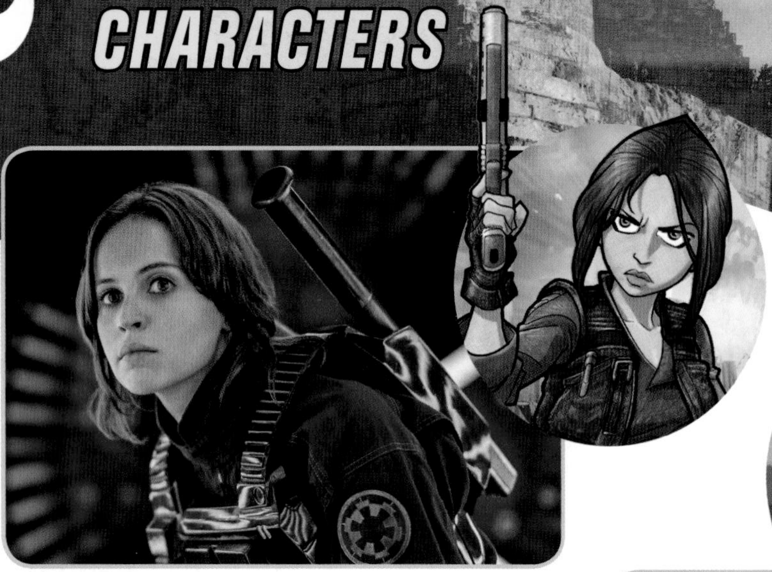

JYN ERSO

Born on planet Vallt to scientists Lyra and Galen Erso, Jyn has become **a fighter, a smuggler and a petty criminal** since she lost her mother to the Empire. Drifting from planet to planet, she doesn't want to get involved with the Rebellion or the Empire. But as rebel leader Mon Mothma believes, she just deserves **a chance to prove that she is on the right side**.

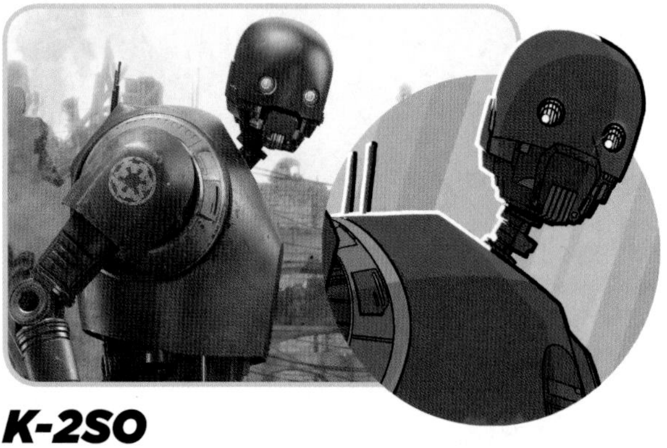

K-2SO

Although he looks like any other Imperial security droid, K-2SO has been personally **reprogrammed by Cassian Andor** and is now fighting alongside the Alliance to restore the Republic. Loyal to its cause, he is an invaluable resource to save the galaxy.

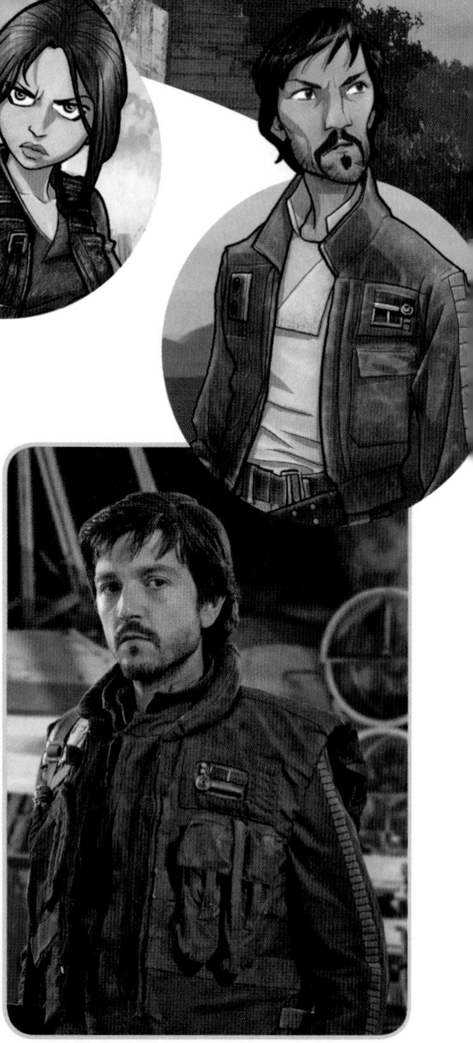

CASSIAN ANDOR

After losing his father at a young age during the Clone Wars, Cassian joined an insurrectionist cell. Recruited by General Draven, he then became **an operative in the Alliance Intelligence**, a saboteur and a spy, often undertaking dangerous missions in direct contact with the Empire.

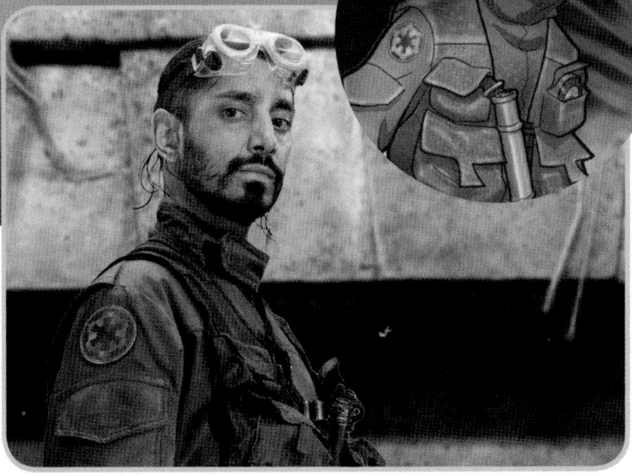
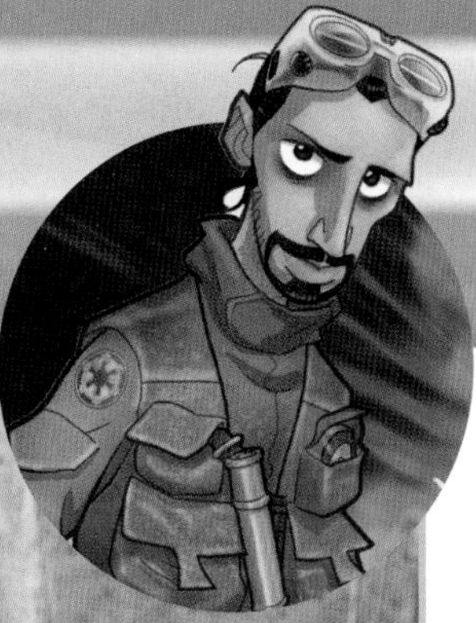

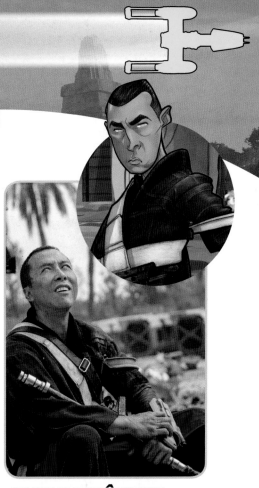

BODHI ROOK

As an **Imperial cargo pilot**, Bodhi Rook used to carry **kyber crystals** from Jedha to a secret base on planet Eadu. But when he meets captive scientist Galen Erso and learns about the existence of the Death Star, his life changes forever: Rook **decides to defect and warn the Rebel Alliance** of the Empire's new weapon.

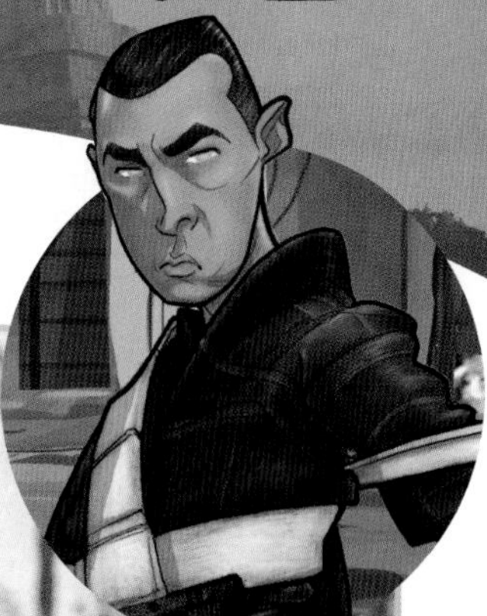
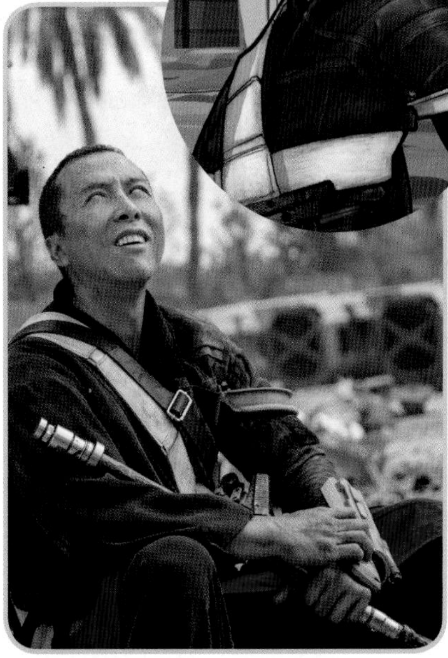

CHIRRUT ÎMWE

A follower of the teachings of the Force, Chirrut Îmwe is a member of the nearly extinct **order of the Guardians of the Whills**—charged with protecting the Temple of the Kyber in the Holy City of Jedha. Despite being blind, Chirrut is an **expert warrior with extraordinary martial arts abilities**.

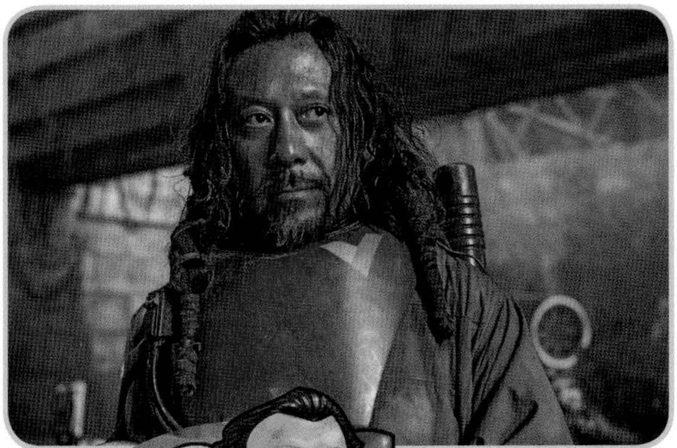
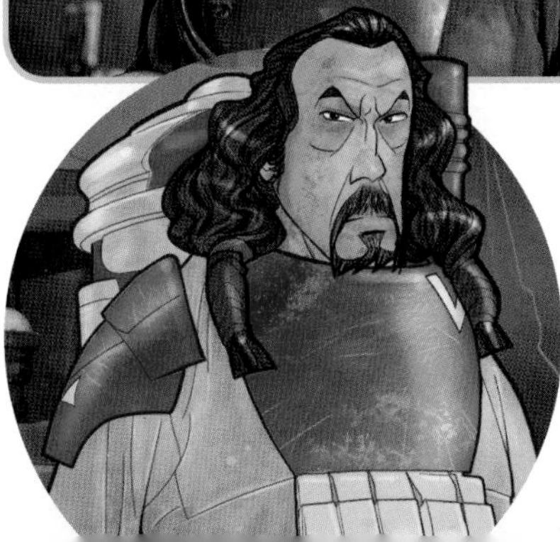

BAZE MALBUS

Once **a Guardian of the Whills**, Baze has lost his faith and left the order, exchanging his vestments for combat armor and a heavy repeating blaster. A veteran **specialized in hit and run tactics**, he never leaves the side of his best friend Chirrut Îmwe.

Meet the CHARACTERS

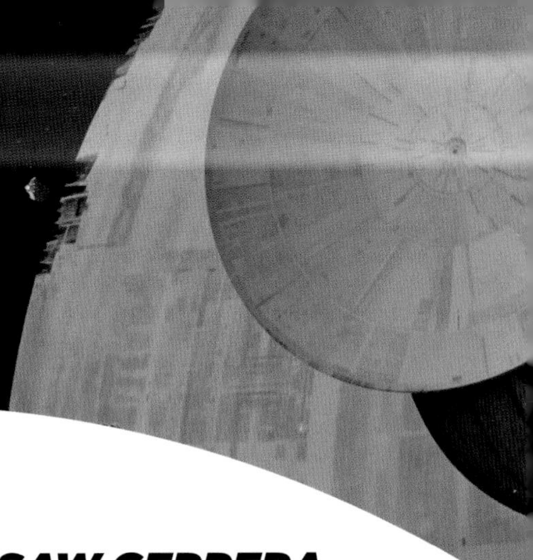

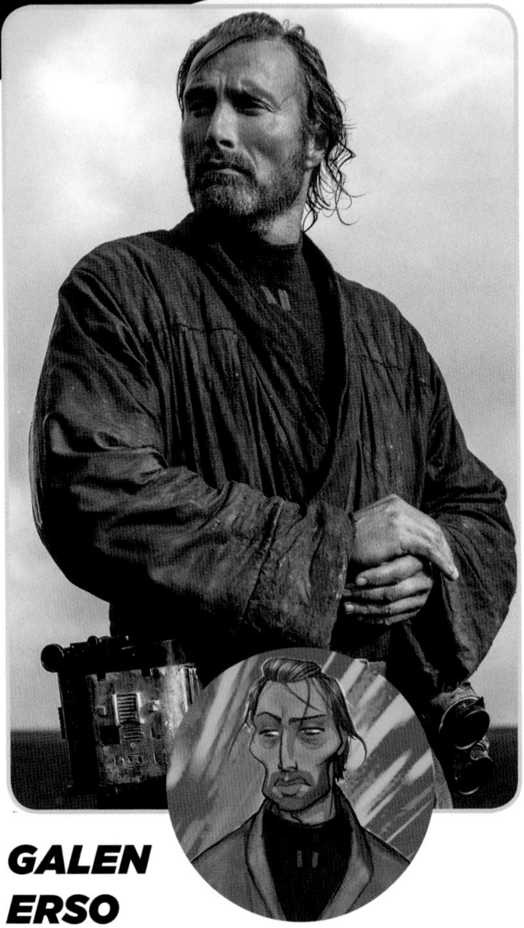

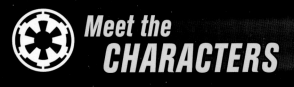

SAW GERRERA

The leader of a feared armed force, **Saw Gerrera only fights to destroy the Empire**. A young resistance fighter during the Clone Wars, Saw is now a veteran warrior who lost not only his compassion, but also his right leg and his health. He now hides in the Catacombs of Cadera on Jedha, gathering information about a devastating Imperial superweapon.

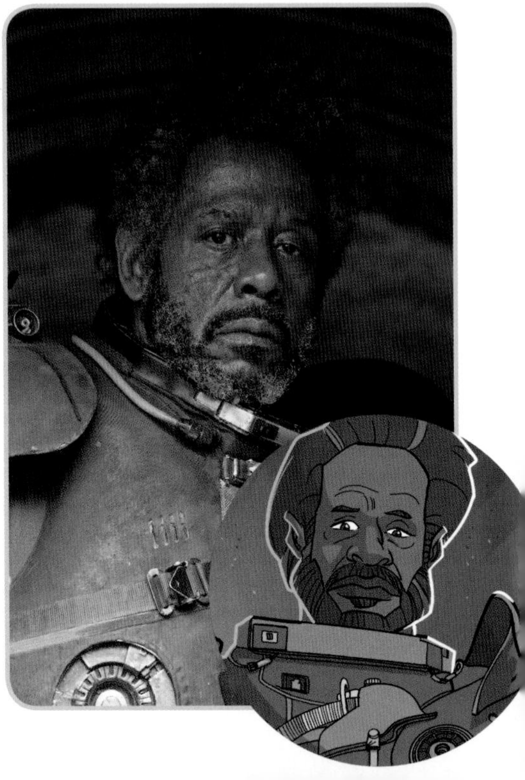

GALEN ERSO

Galen Erso has been **the brilliant mind behind Project Celestial Power**—intended to provide sustainable energy for remote worlds. When he finds out that his friend Orson Krennic is using **his discoveries on kyber crystals to weaponize the Death Star**, Galen flees to planet Lah'mu with his family. Unfortunately, the Empire has found them.

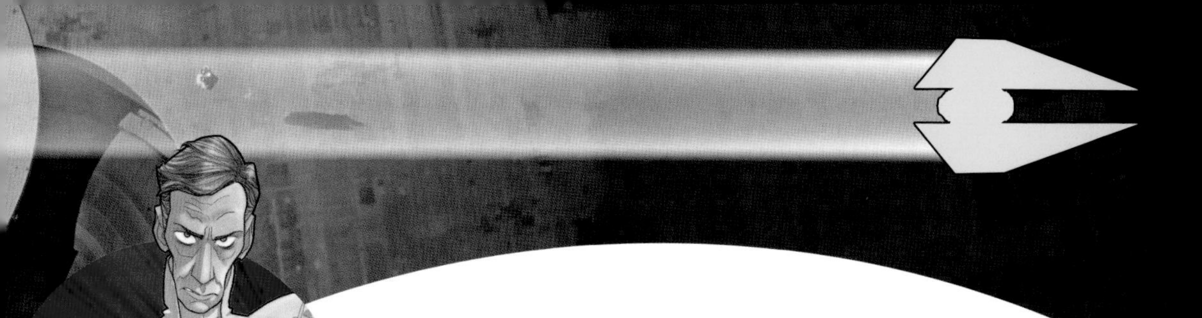

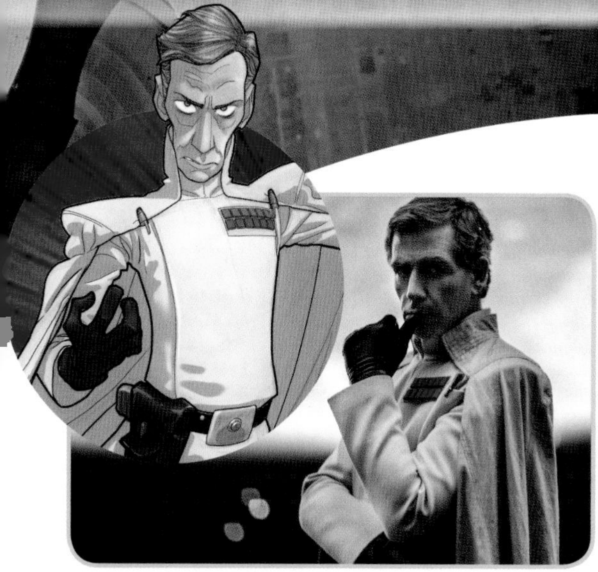

GOVERNOR TARKIN

Regional Governor of the Outer Rim, Tarkin is a high-ranking Imperial officer **sent to supervise the test of the superweapon built by Orson Krennic**. Loyal to the Emperor, Tarkin believes that the terror caused by a fully operational Death Star will ensure peace throughout the Galaxy.

ORSON KRENNIC

Ruthless and ambitious, Orson Krennic is always trying to prove himself to the Emperor. He finally gets a chance when he becomes **Director of Advanced Weapons Research**, responsible for the construction of the Death Star.

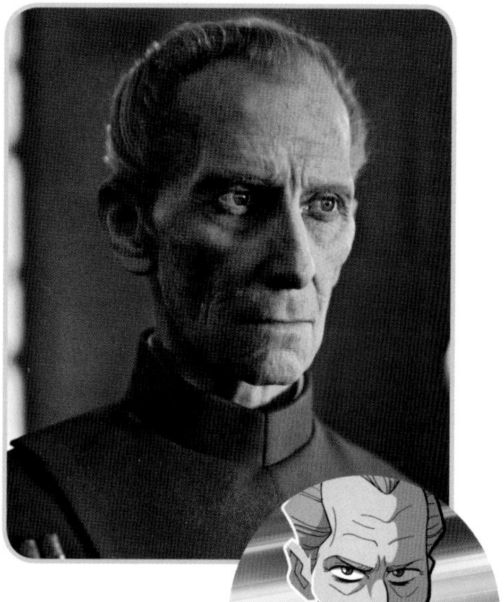

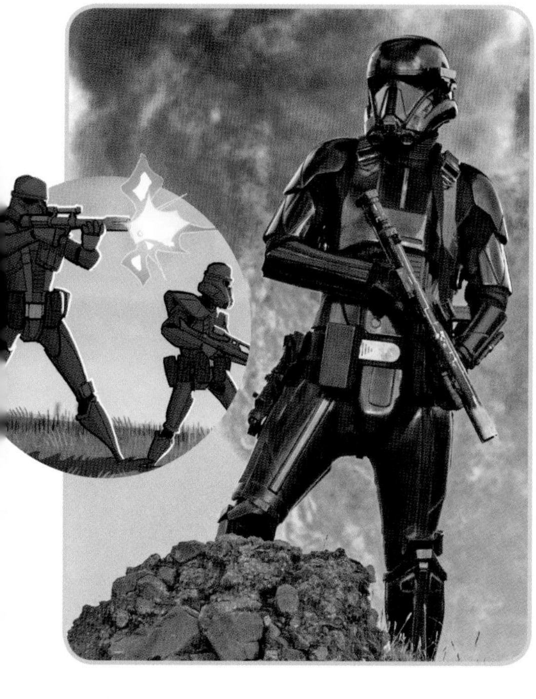

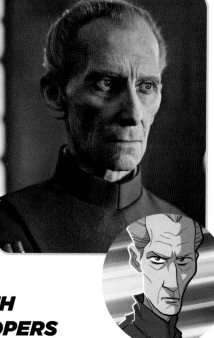

DEATH TROOPERS

Recruited by the Imperial Intelligence to protect the most important Imperial operations, Death Troopers are **stronger, faster and more lethal than other soldiers**. Krennic considers these elite stormtroopers his personal guard and doesn't make a move without them.

"SAW GERRERA USED TO SAY... ONE FIGHTER WITH A SHARP STICK AND NOTHING LEFT TO LOSE CAN TAKE THE DAY."

JYN ERSO

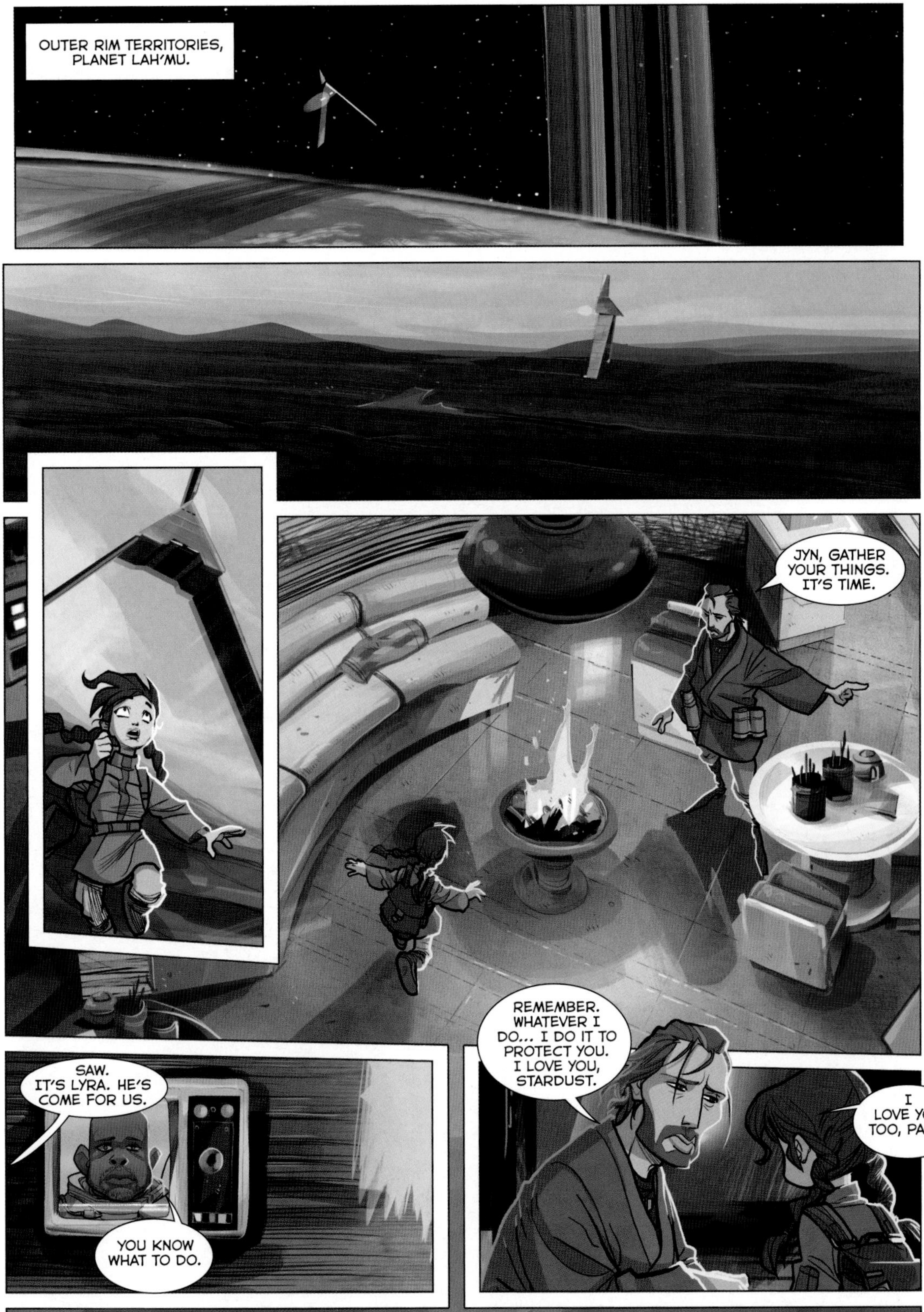
OUTER RIM TERRITORIES, PLANET LAH'MU.
JYN, GATHER YOUR THINGS. IT'S TIME.
SAW. IT'S LYRA. HE'S COME FOR US.
YOU KNOW WHAT TO DO.
REMEMBER. WHATEVER I DO... I DO IT TO PROTECT YOU. I LOVE YOU, STARDUST.
I LOVE YOU TOO, PAPA.

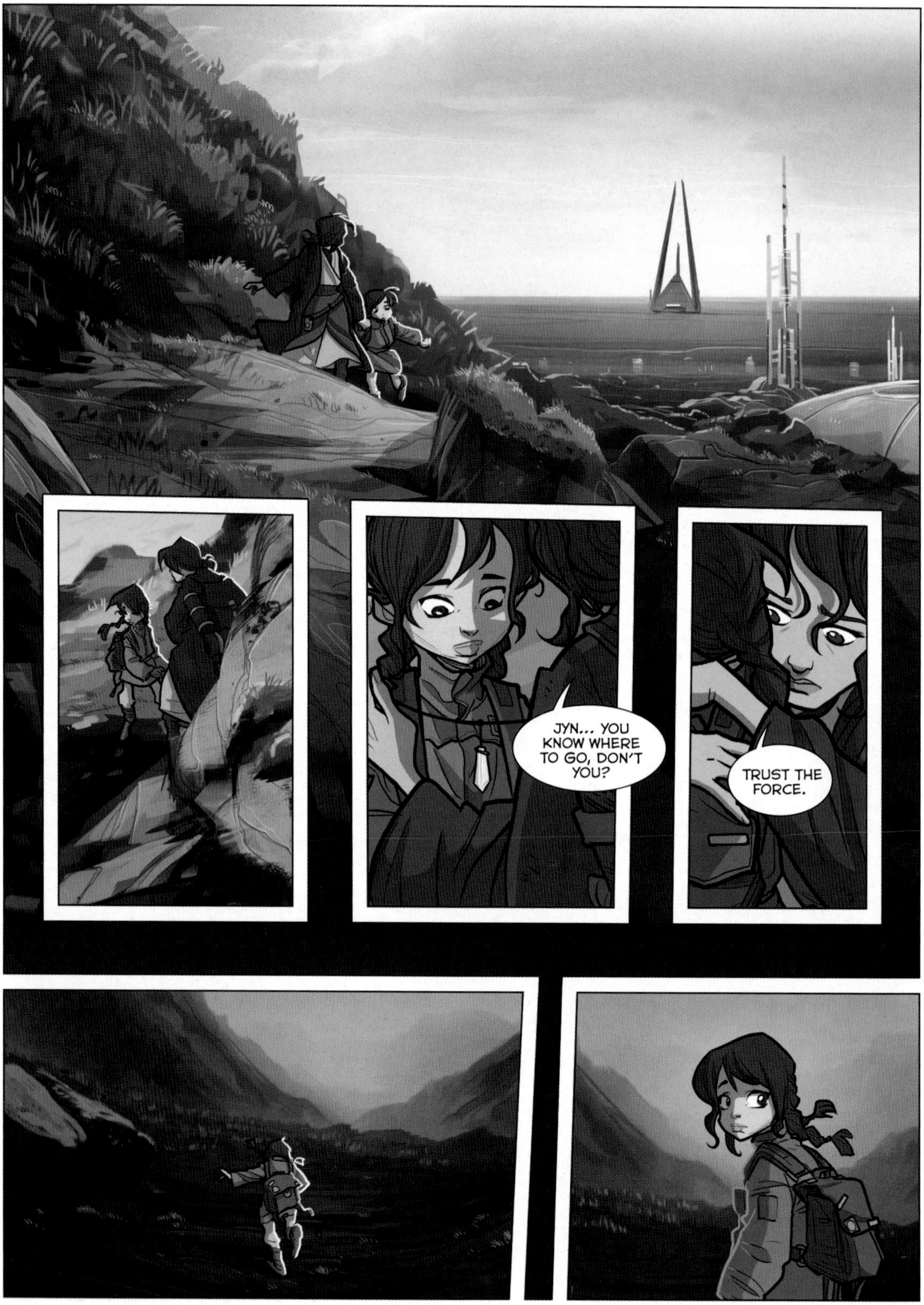
JYN... YOU KNOW WHERE TO GO, DON'T YOU?
TRUST THE FORCE.

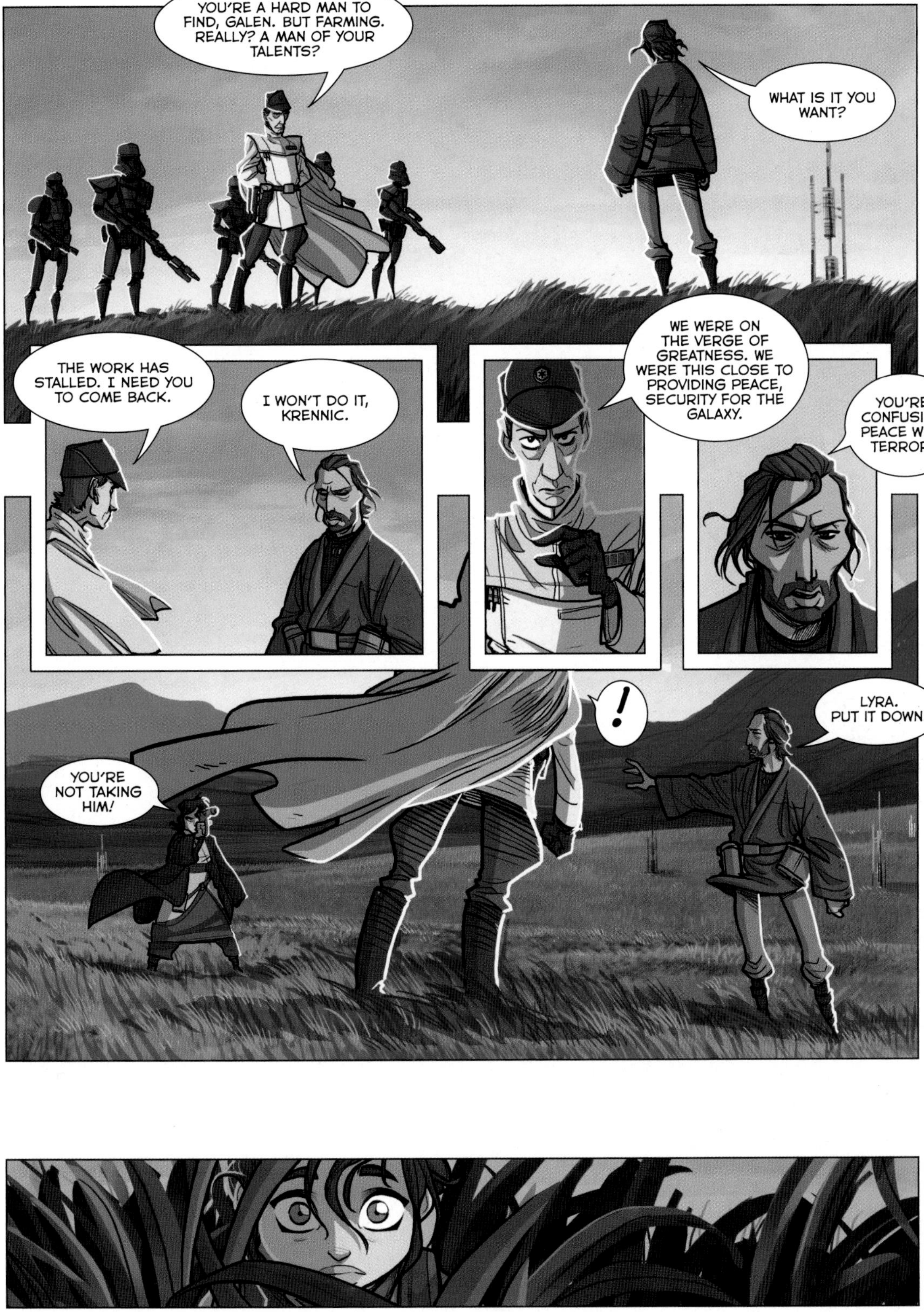
YOU'RE A HARD MAN TO FIND, GALEN. BUT FARMING. REALLY? A MAN OF YOUR TALENTS?
WHAT IS IT YOU WANT?
THE WORK HAS STALLED. I NEED YOU TO COME BACK.
I WON'T DO IT, KRENNIC.
WE WERE ON THE VERGE OF GREATNESS. WE WERE THIS CLOSE TO PROVIDING PEACE, SECURITY FOR THE GALAXY.
YOU'RE CONFUSING PEACE WITH TERROR.
!
LYRA. PUT IT DOWN.
YOU'RE NOT TAKING HIM!

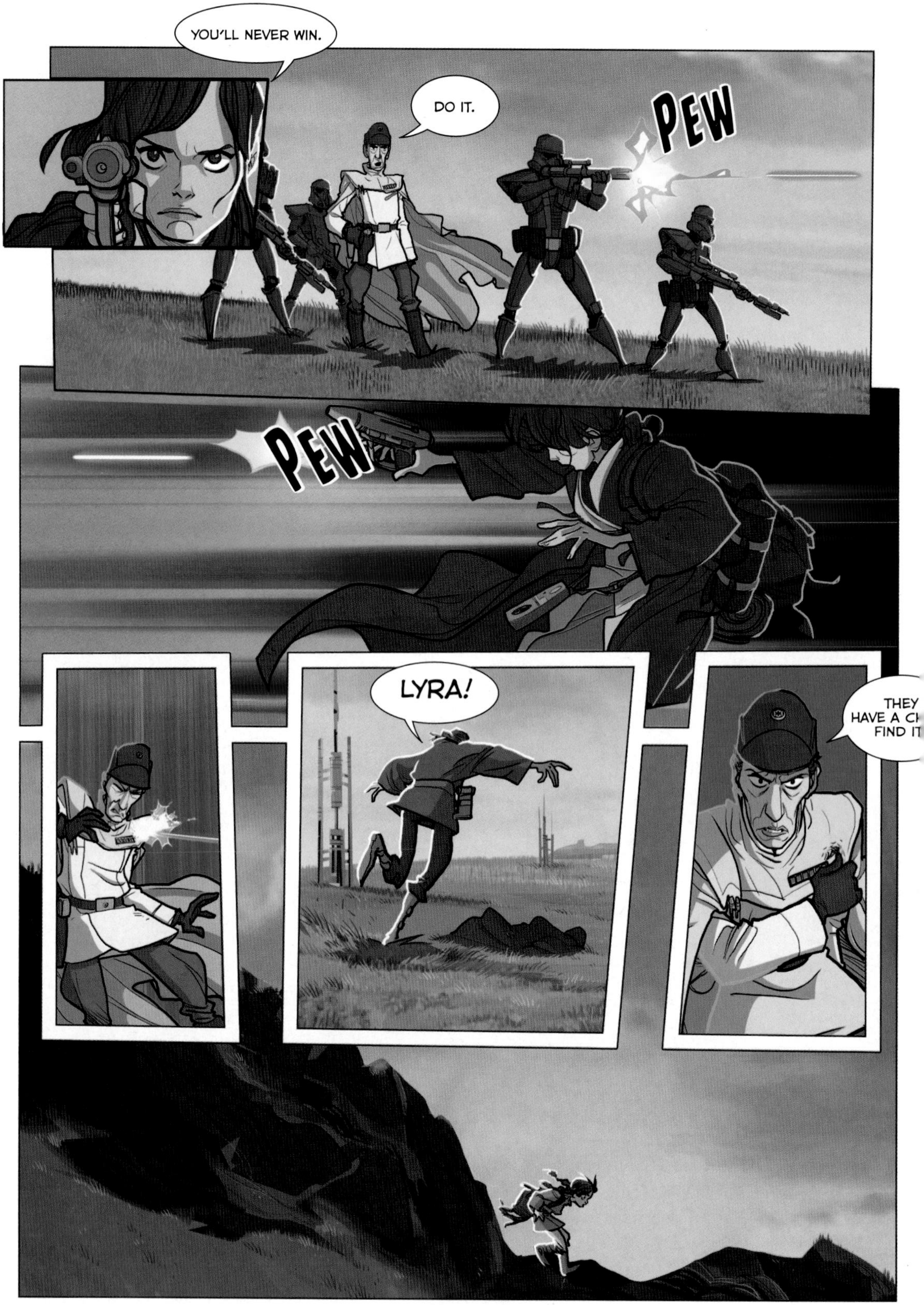
YOU'LL NEVER WIN.
DO IT.
PEW
PEW
LYRA!
THEY HAVE A C FIND IT

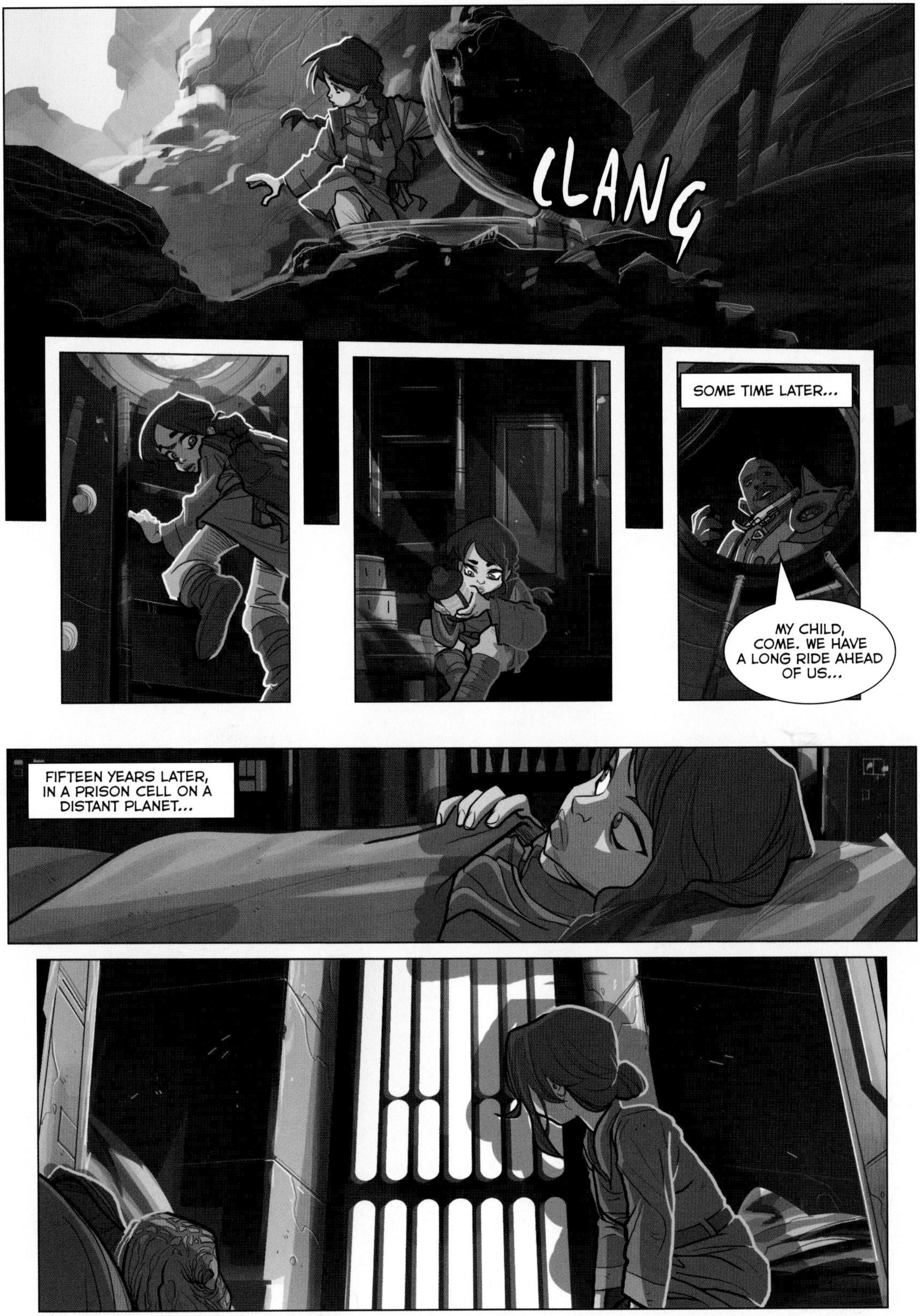
CLANG
SOME TIME LATER...
MY CHILD, COME. WE HAVE A LONG RIDE AHEAD OF US...
FIFTEEN YEARS LATER, IN A PRISON CELL ON A DISTANT PLANET...

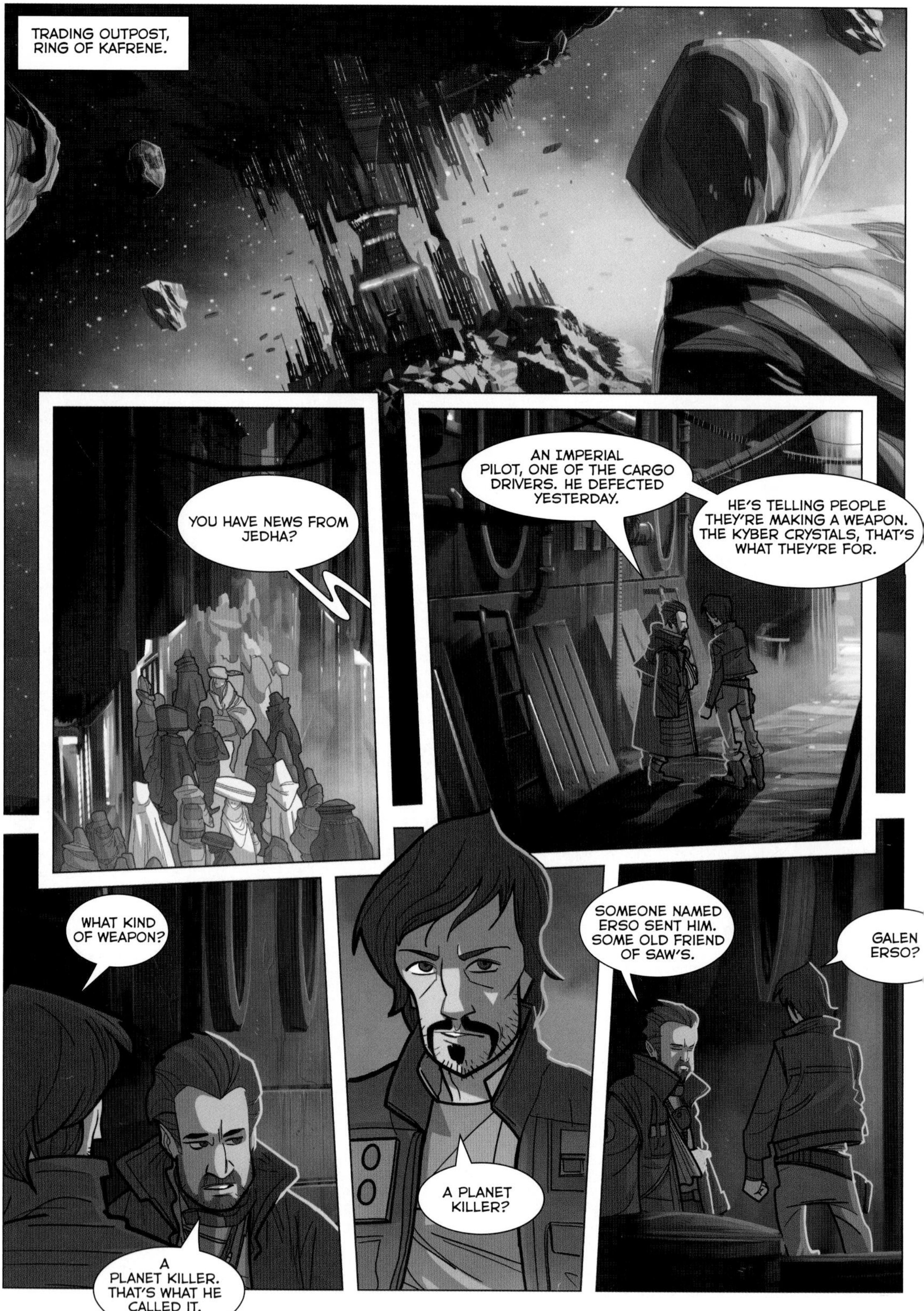

TRADING OUTPOST, RING OF KAFRENE.
YOU HAVE NEWS FROM JEDHA?
AN IMPERIAL PILOT, ONE OF THE CARGO DRIVERS. HE DEFECTED YESTERDAY.
HE'S TELLING PEOPLE THEY'RE MAKING A WEAPON. THE KYBER CRYSTALS, THAT'S WHAT THEY'RE FOR.
WHAT KIND OF WEAPON?
A PLANET KILLER. THAT'S WHAT HE CALLED IT.
A PLANET KILLER?
SOMEONE NAMED ERSO SENT HIM. SOME OLD FRIEND OF SAW'S.
GALEN ERSO?

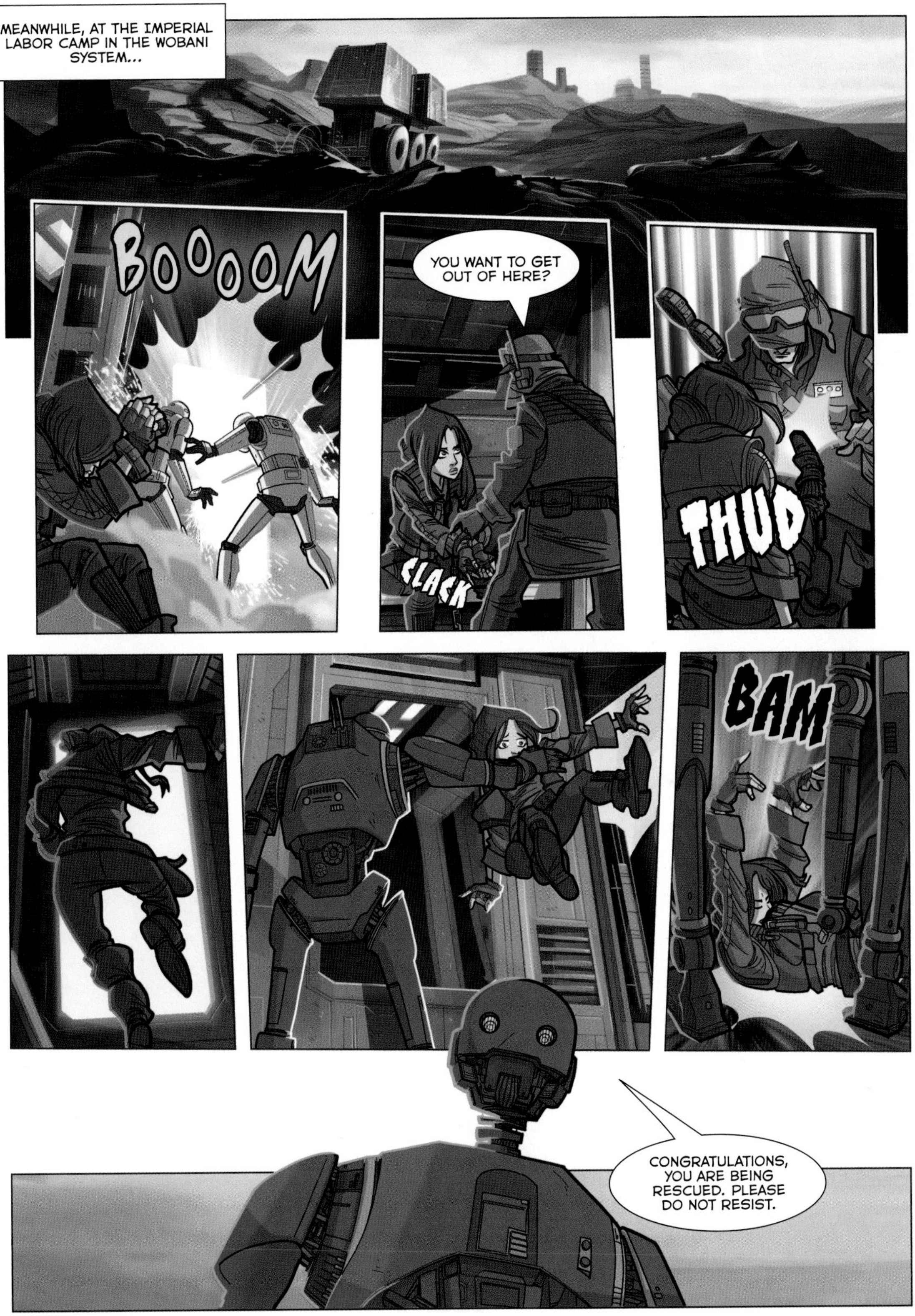

MEANWHILE, AT THE IMPERIAL LABOR CAMP IN THE WOBANI SYSTEM...
BOOOOM
YOU WANT TO GET OUT OF HERE?
CLACK
THUD
BAM
CONGRATULATIONS, YOU ARE BEING RESCUED. PLEASE DO NOT RESIST.

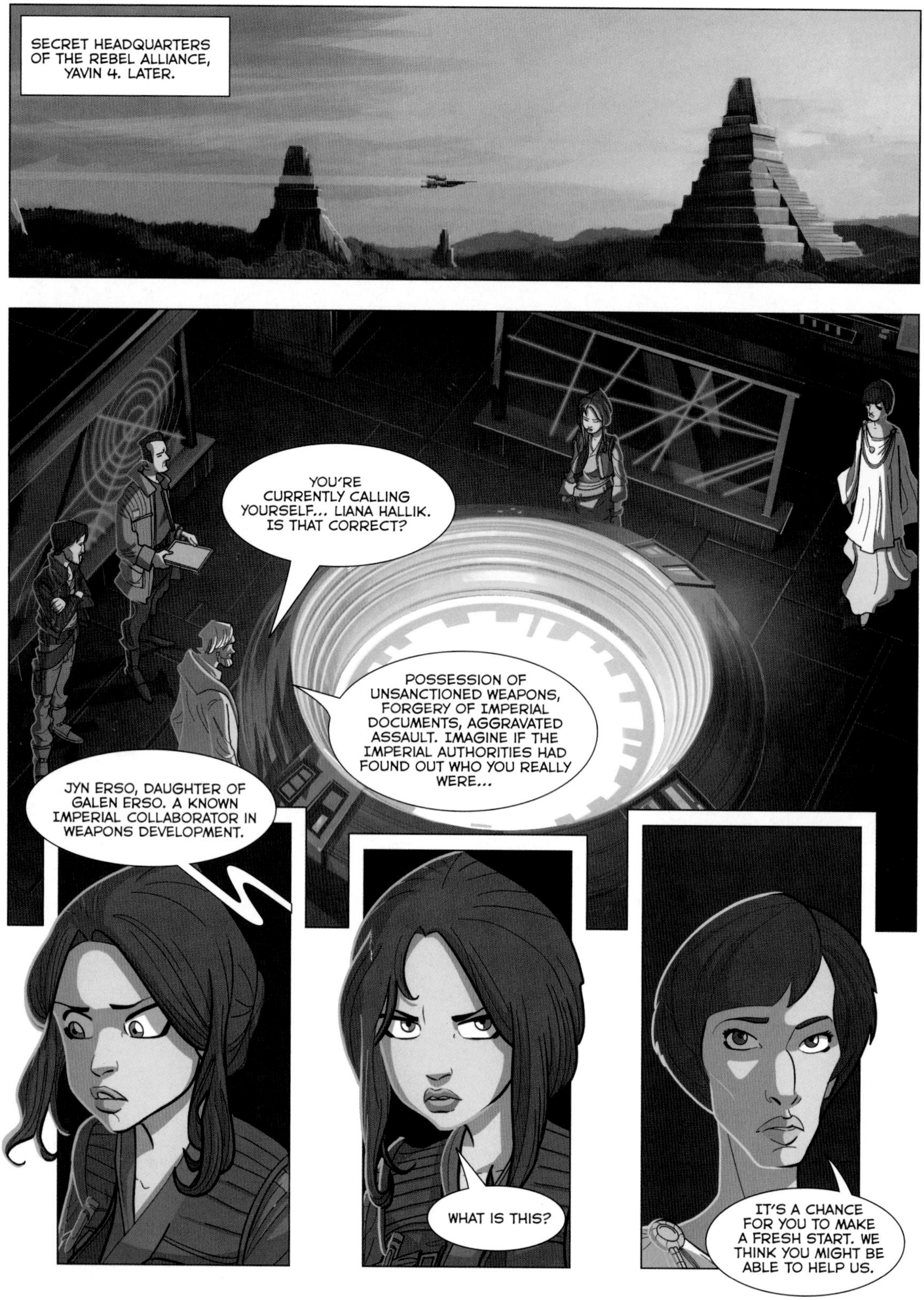
SECRET HEADQUARTERS OF THE REBEL ALLIANCE, YAVIN 4. LATER.
YOU'RE CURRENTLY CALLING YOURSELF... LIANA HALLIK. IS THAT CORRECT?
POSSESSION OF UNSANCTIONED WEAPONS, FORGERY OF IMPERIAL DOCUMENTS, AGGRAVATED ASSAULT. IMAGINE IF THE IMPERIAL AUTHORITIES HAD FOUND OUT WHO YOU REALLY WERE...
JYN ERSO, DAUGHTER OF GALEN ERSO. A KNOWN IMPERIAL COLLABORATOR IN WEAPONS DEVELOPMENT.
WHAT IS THIS?
IT'S A CHANCE FOR YOU TO MAKE A FRESH START. WE THINK YOU MIGHT BE ABLE TO HELP US.

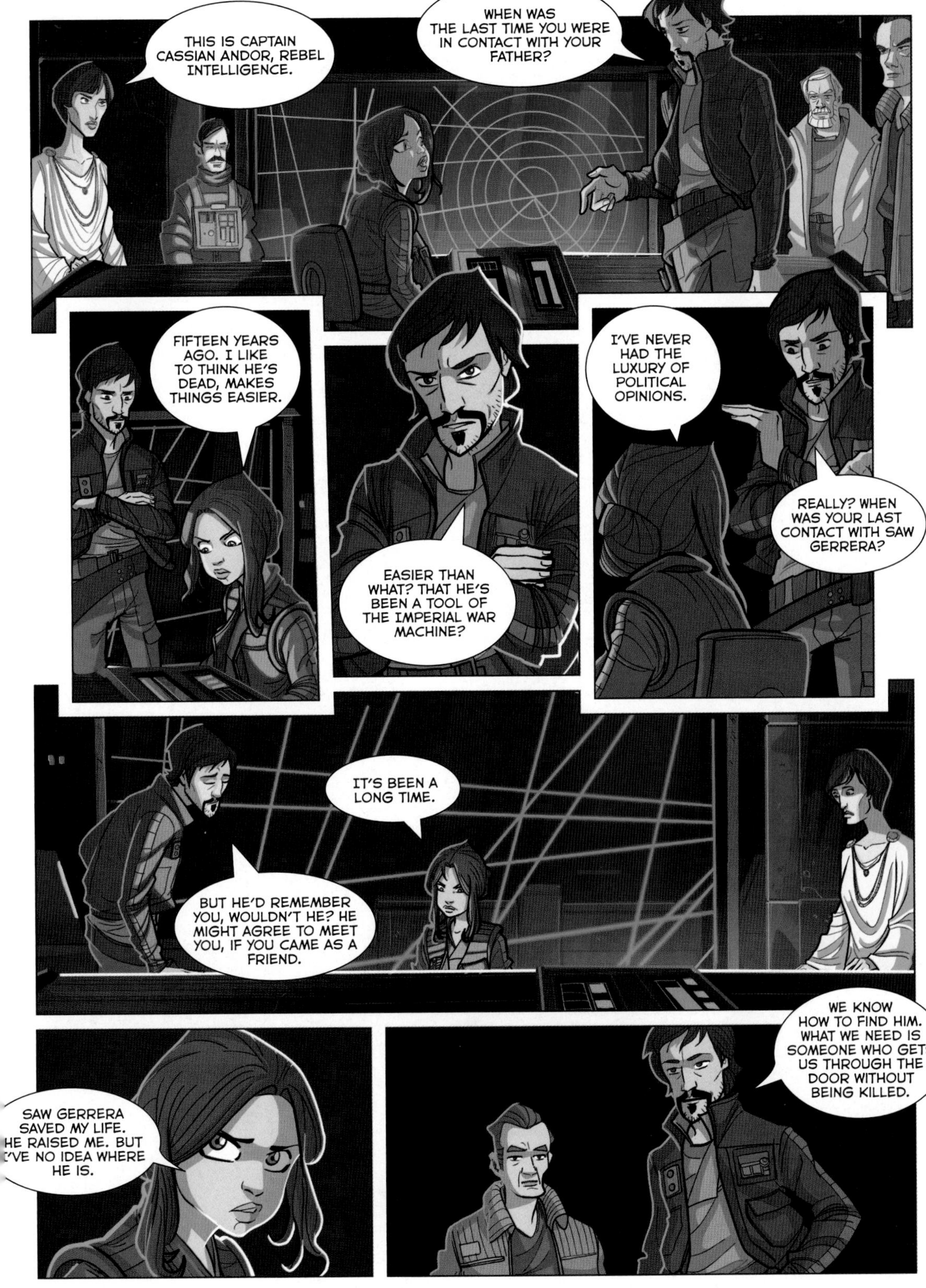
THIS IS CAPTAIN CASSIAN ANDOR, REBEL INTELLIGENCE.
WHEN WAS THE LAST TIME YOU WERE IN CONTACT WITH YOUR FATHER?
FIFTEEN YEARS AGO. I LIKE TO THINK HE'S DEAD, MAKES THINGS EASIER.
EASIER THAN WHAT? THAT HE'S BEEN A TOOL OF THE IMPERIAL WAR MACHINE?
I'VE NEVER HAD THE LUXURY OF POLITICAL OPINIONS.
REALLY? WHEN WAS YOUR LAST CONTACT WITH SAW GERRERA?
IT'S BEEN A LONG TIME.
BUT HE'D REMEMBER YOU, WOULDN'T HE? HE MIGHT AGREE TO MEET YOU, IF YOU CAME AS A FRIEND.
SAW GERRERA SAVED MY LIFE. HE RAISED ME. BUT I'VE NO IDEA WHERE HE IS.
WE KNOW HOW TO FIND HIM. WHAT WE NEED IS SOMEONE WHO GETS US THROUGH THE DOOR WITHOUT BEING KILLED.

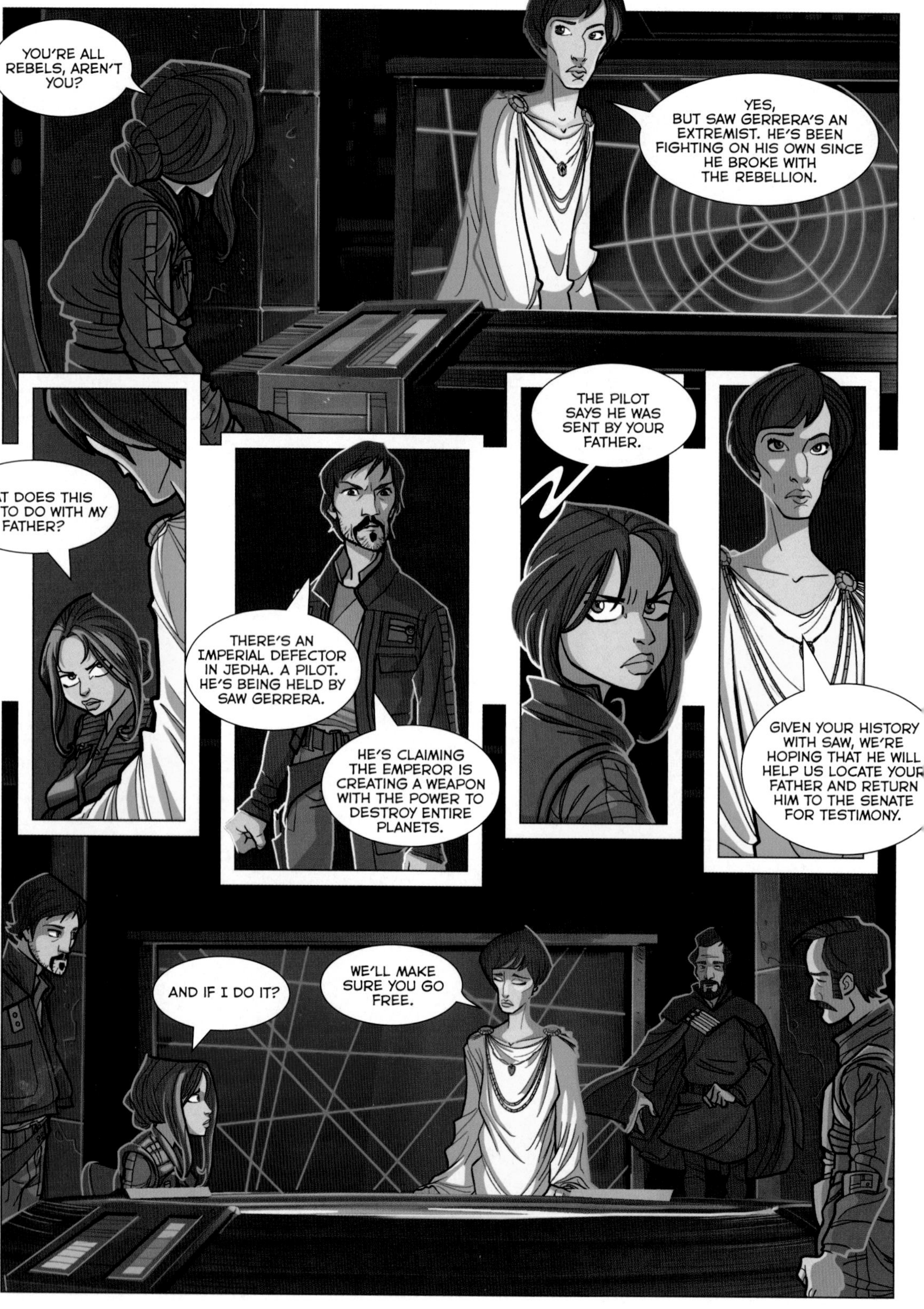
YOU'RE ALL REBELS, AREN'T YOU?
YES, BUT SAW GERRERA'S AN EXTREMIST. HE'S BEEN FIGHTING ON HIS OWN SINCE HE BROKE WITH THE REBELLION.
WHAT DOES THIS HAVE TO DO WITH MY FATHER?
THERE'S AN IMPERIAL DEFECTOR IN JEDHA. A PILOT. HE'S BEING HELD BY SAW GERRERA.
HE'S CLAIMING THE EMPEROR IS CREATING A WEAPON WITH THE POWER TO DESTROY ENTIRE PLANETS.
THE PILOT SAYS HE WAS SENT BY YOUR FATHER.
GIVEN YOUR HISTORY WITH SAW, WE'RE HOPING THAT HE WILL HELP US LOCATE YOUR FATHER AND RETURN HIM TO THE SENATE FOR TESTIMONY.
AND IF I DO IT?
WE'LL MAKE SURE YOU GO FREE.

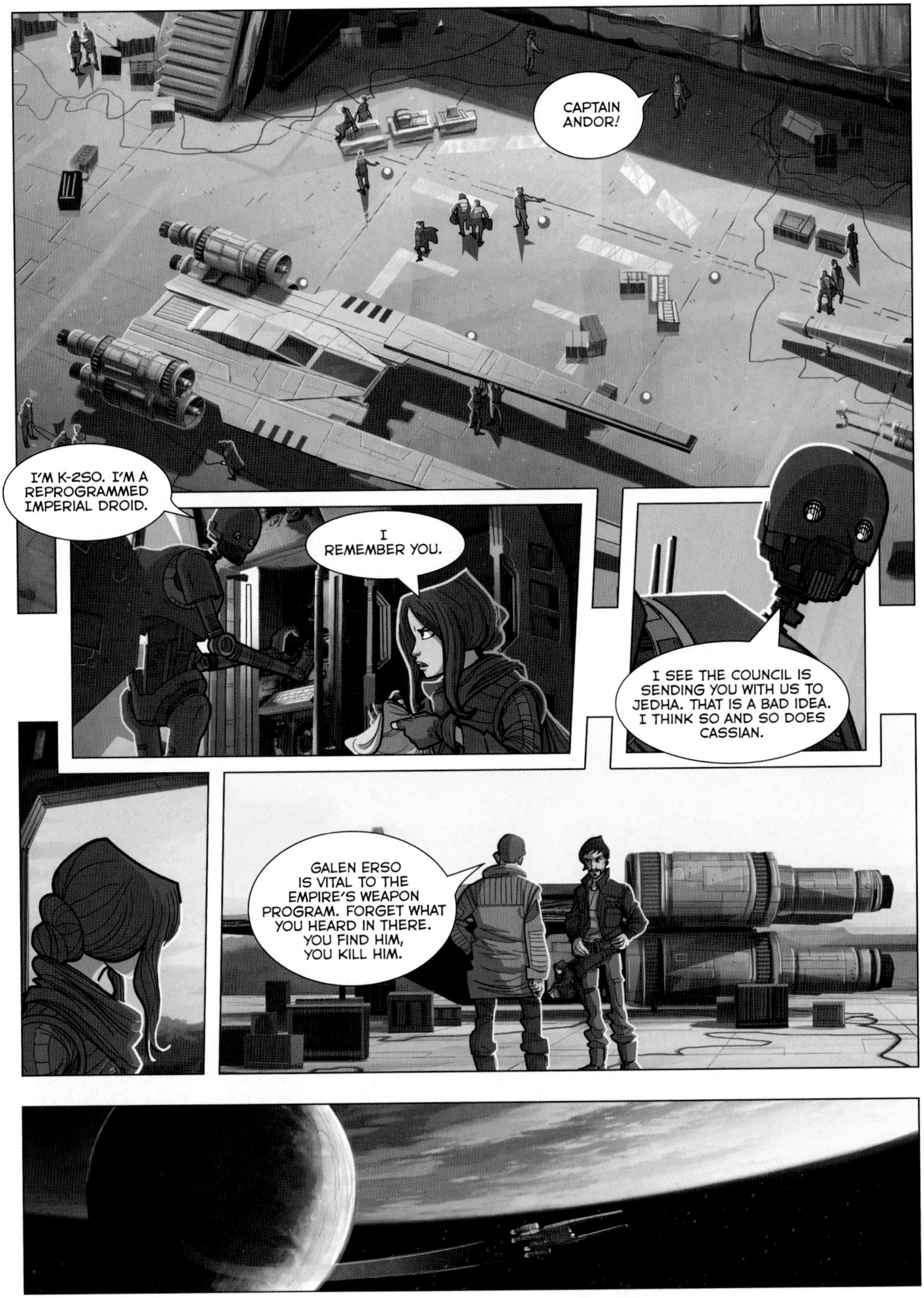
CAPTAIN ANDOR!
I'M K-2SO. I'M A REPROGRAMMED IMPERIAL DROID.
I REMEMBER YOU.
I SEE THE COUNCIL IS SENDING YOU WITH US TO JEDHA. THAT IS A BAD IDEA. I THINK SO AND SO DOES CASSIAN.
GALEN ERSO IS VITAL TO THE EMPIRE'S WEAPON PROGRAM. FORGET WHAT YOU HEARD IN THERE. YOU FIND HIM, YOU KILL HIM.

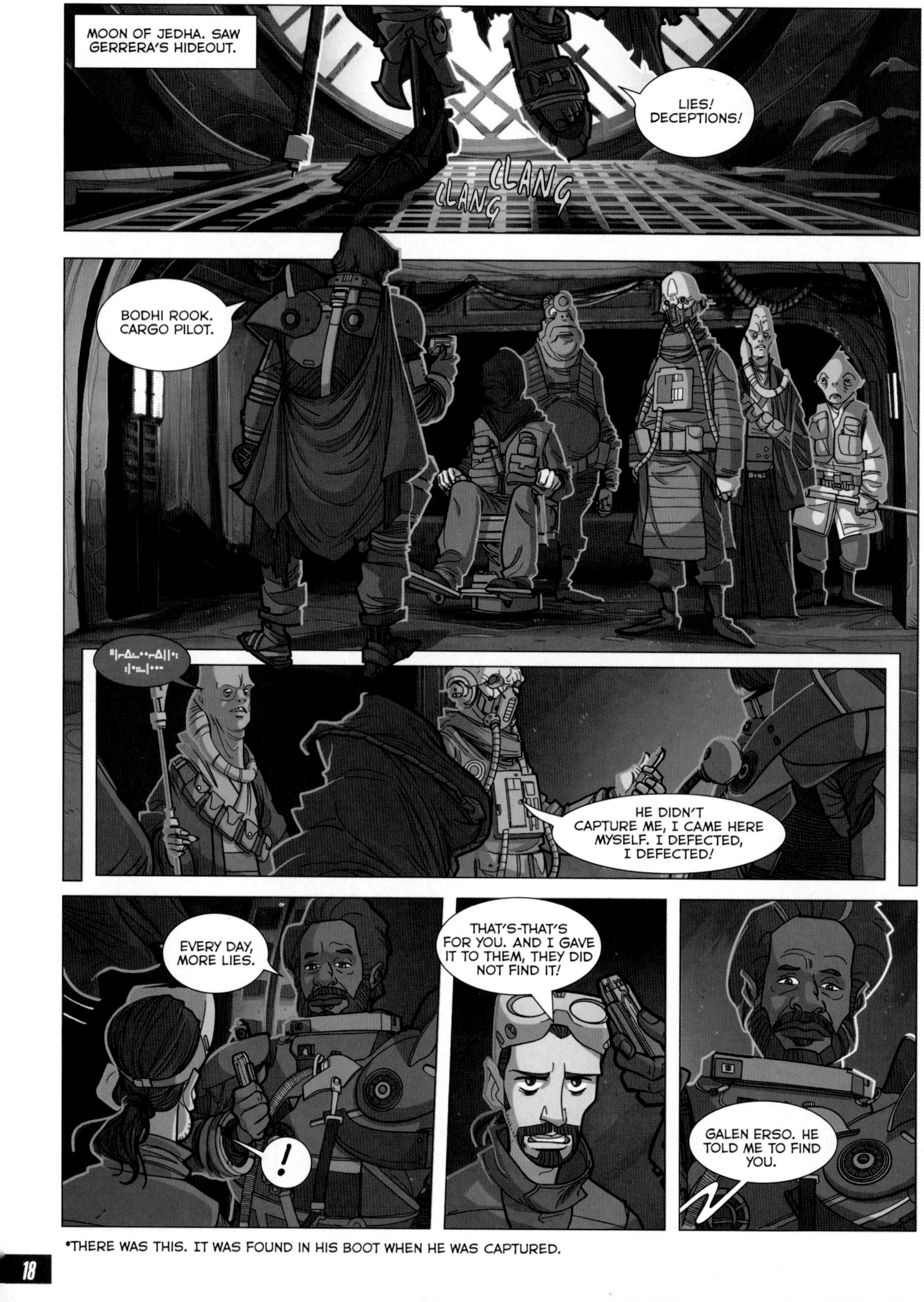
MOON OF JEDHA. SAW GERRERA'S HIDEOUT.
LIES! DECEPTIONS!
CLANG CLANG
BODHI ROOK. CARGO PILOT.
HE DIDN'T CAPTURE ME, I CAME HERE MYSELF. I DEFECTED, I DEFECTED!
EVERY DAY, MORE LIES.
!
THAT'S-THAT'S FOR YOU. AND I GAVE IT TO THEM, THEY DID NOT FIND IT!
GALEN ERSO. HE TOLD ME TO FIND YOU.

*THERE WAS THIS. IT WAS FOUND IN HIS BOOT WHEN HE WAS CAPTURED.

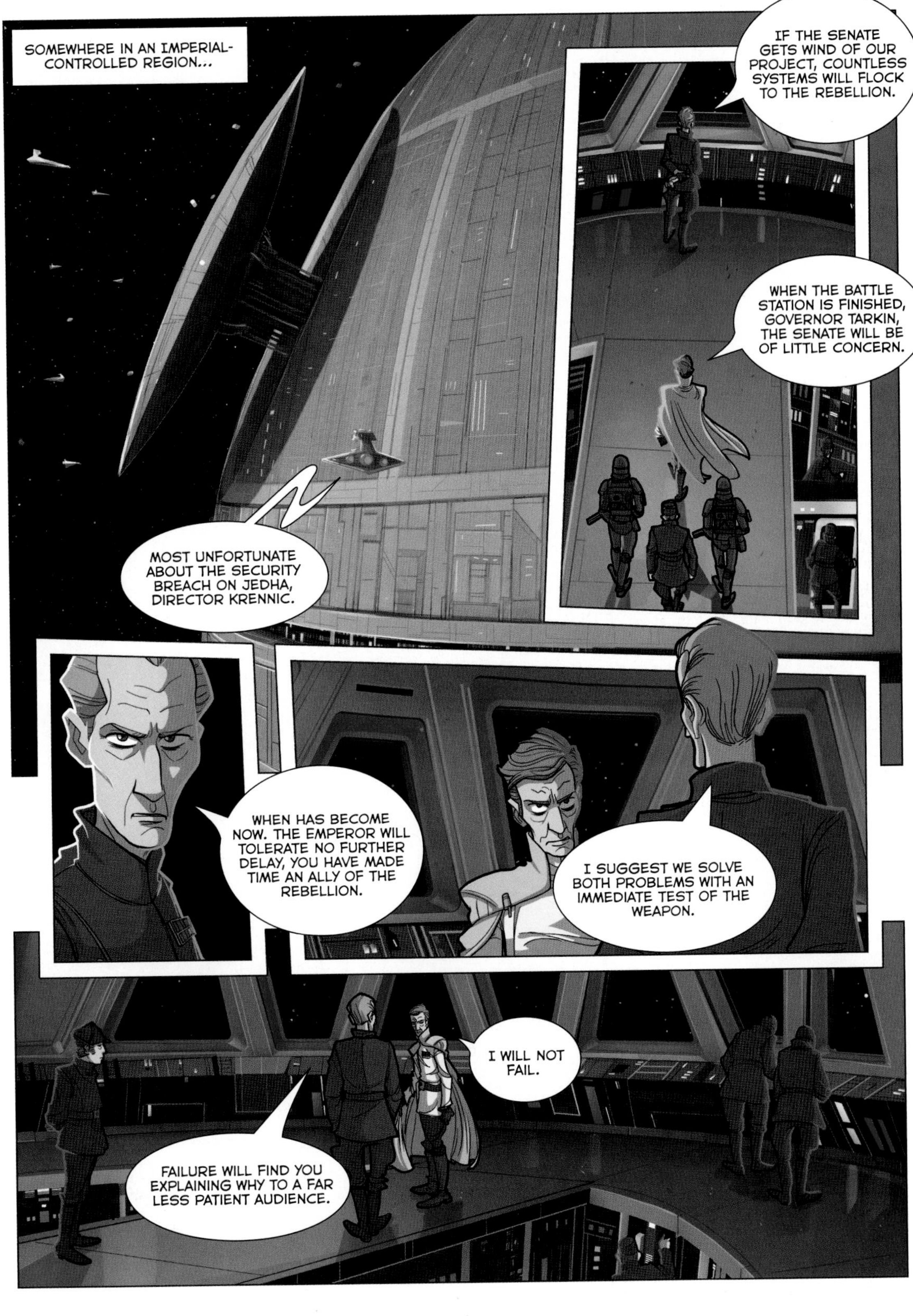
SOMEWHERE IN AN IMPERIAL-CONTROLLED REGION...
MOST UNFORTUNATE ABOUT THE SECURITY BREACH ON JEDHA, DIRECTOR KRENNIC.
IF THE SENATE GETS WIND OF OUR PROJECT, COUNTLESS SYSTEMS WILL FLOCK TO THE REBELLION.
WHEN THE BATTLE STATION IS FINISHED, GOVERNOR TARKIN, THE SENATE WILL BE OF LITTLE CONCERN.
WHEN HAS BECOME NOW. THE EMPEROR WILL TOLERATE NO FURTHER DELAY, YOU HAVE MADE TIME AN ALLY OF THE REBELLION.
I SUGGEST WE SOLVE BOTH PROBLEMS WITH AN IMMEDIATE TEST OF THE WEAPON.
I WILL NOT FAIL.
FAILURE WILL FIND YOU EXPLAINING WHY TO A FAR LESS PATIENT AUDIENCE.

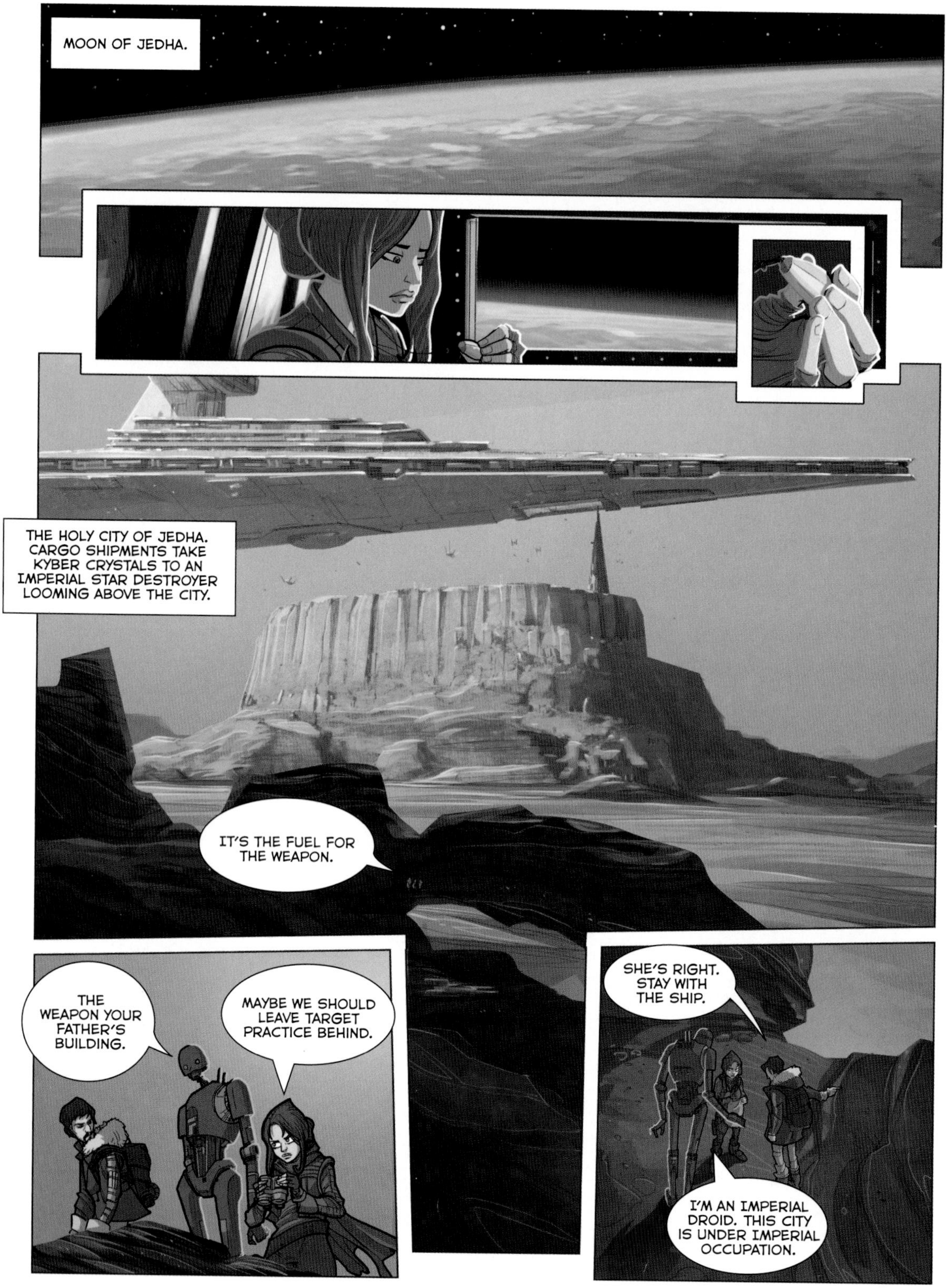

MOON OF JEDHA.
THE HOLY CITY OF JEDHA. CARGO SHIPMENTS TAKE KYBER CRYSTALS TO AN IMPERIAL STAR DESTROYER LOOMING ABOVE THE CITY.
IT'S THE FUEL FOR THE WEAPON.
THE WEAPON YOUR FATHER'S BUILDING.
MAYBE WE SHOULD LEAVE TARGET PRACTICE BEHIND.
SHE'S RIGHT. STAY WITH THE SHIP.
I'M AN IMPERIAL DROID. THIS CITY IS UNDER IMPERIAL OCCUPATION.

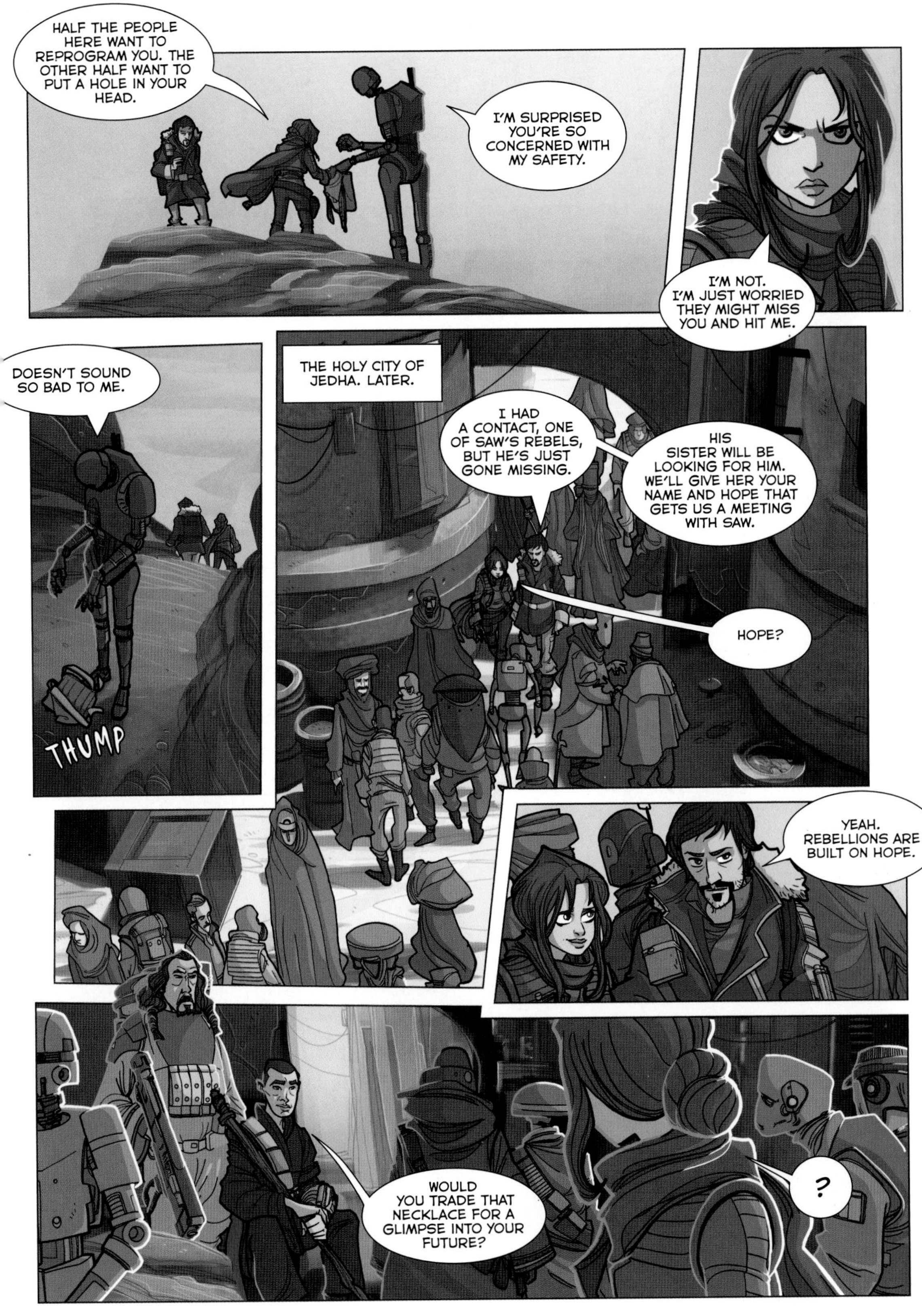

HALF THE PEOPLE HERE WANT TO REPROGRAM YOU. THE OTHER HALF WANT TO PUT A HOLE IN YOUR HEAD.
I'M SURPRISED YOU'RE SO CONCERNED WITH MY SAFETY.
I'M NOT. I'M JUST WORRIED THEY MIGHT MISS YOU AND HIT ME.
DOESN'T SOUND SO BAD TO ME.
THUMP
THE HOLY CITY OF JEDHA. LATER.
I HAD A CONTACT, ONE OF SAW'S REBELS, BUT HE'S JUST GONE MISSING.
HIS SISTER WILL BE LOOKING FOR HIM. WE'LL GIVE HER YOUR NAME AND HOPE THAT GETS US A MEETING WITH SAW.
HOPE?
YEAH. REBELLIONS ARE BUILT ON HOPE.
WOULD YOU TRADE THAT NECKLACE FOR A GLIMPSE INTO YOUR FUTURE?
?

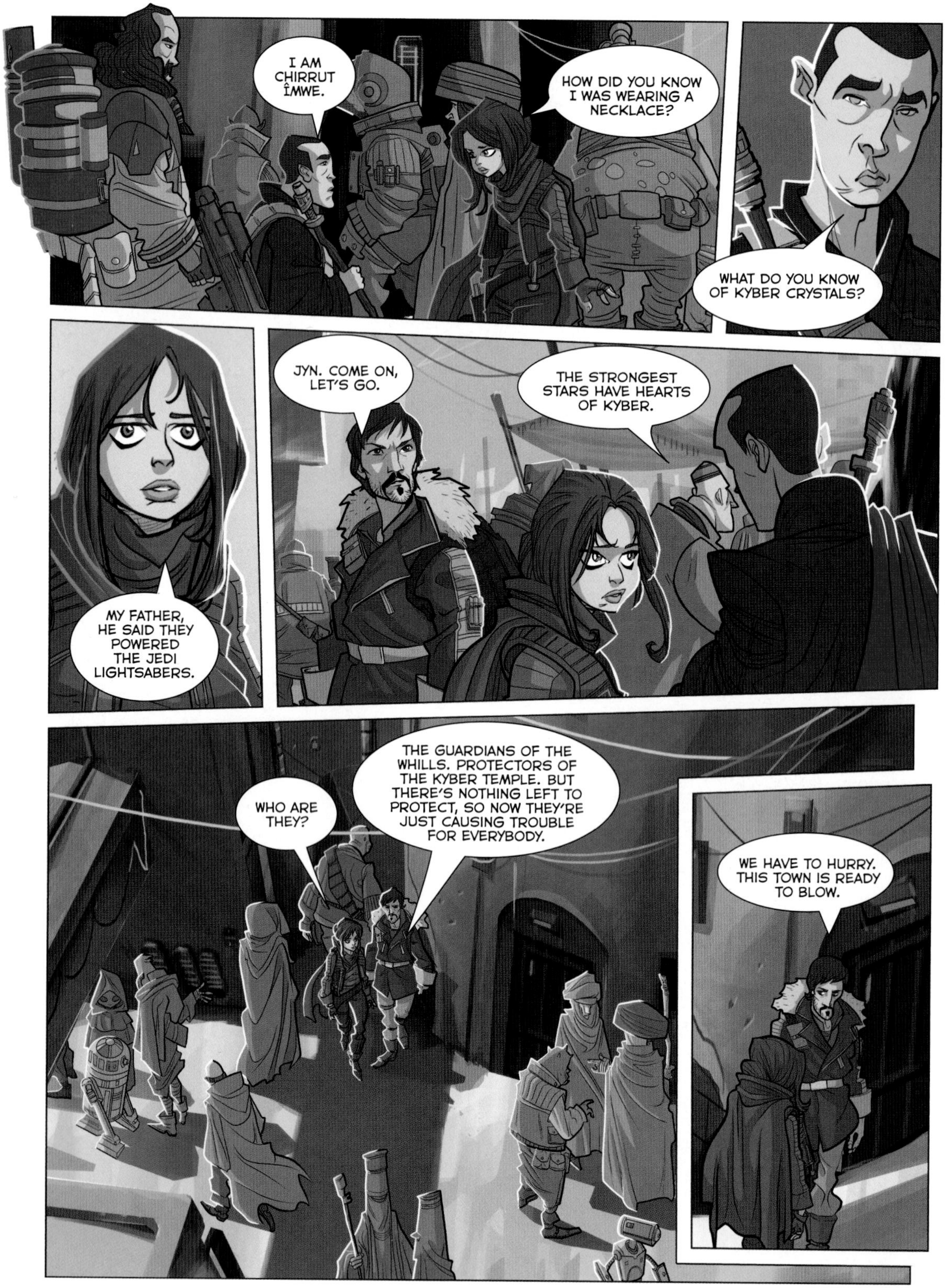
I AM CHIRRUT ÎMWE.
HOW DID YOU KNOW I WAS WEARING A NECKLACE?
WHAT DO YOU KNOW OF KYBER CRYSTALS?
MY FATHER, HE SAID THEY POWERED THE JEDI LIGHTSABERS.
JYN. COME ON, LET'S GO.
THE STRONGEST STARS HAVE HEARTS OF KYBER.
WHO ARE THEY?
THE GUARDIANS OF THE WHILLS. PROTECTORS OF THE KYBER TEMPLE. BUT THERE'S NOTHING LEFT TO PROTECT, SO NOW THEY'RE JUST CAUSING TROUBLE FOR EVERYBODY.
WE HAVE TO HURRY. THIS TOWN IS READY TO BLOW.

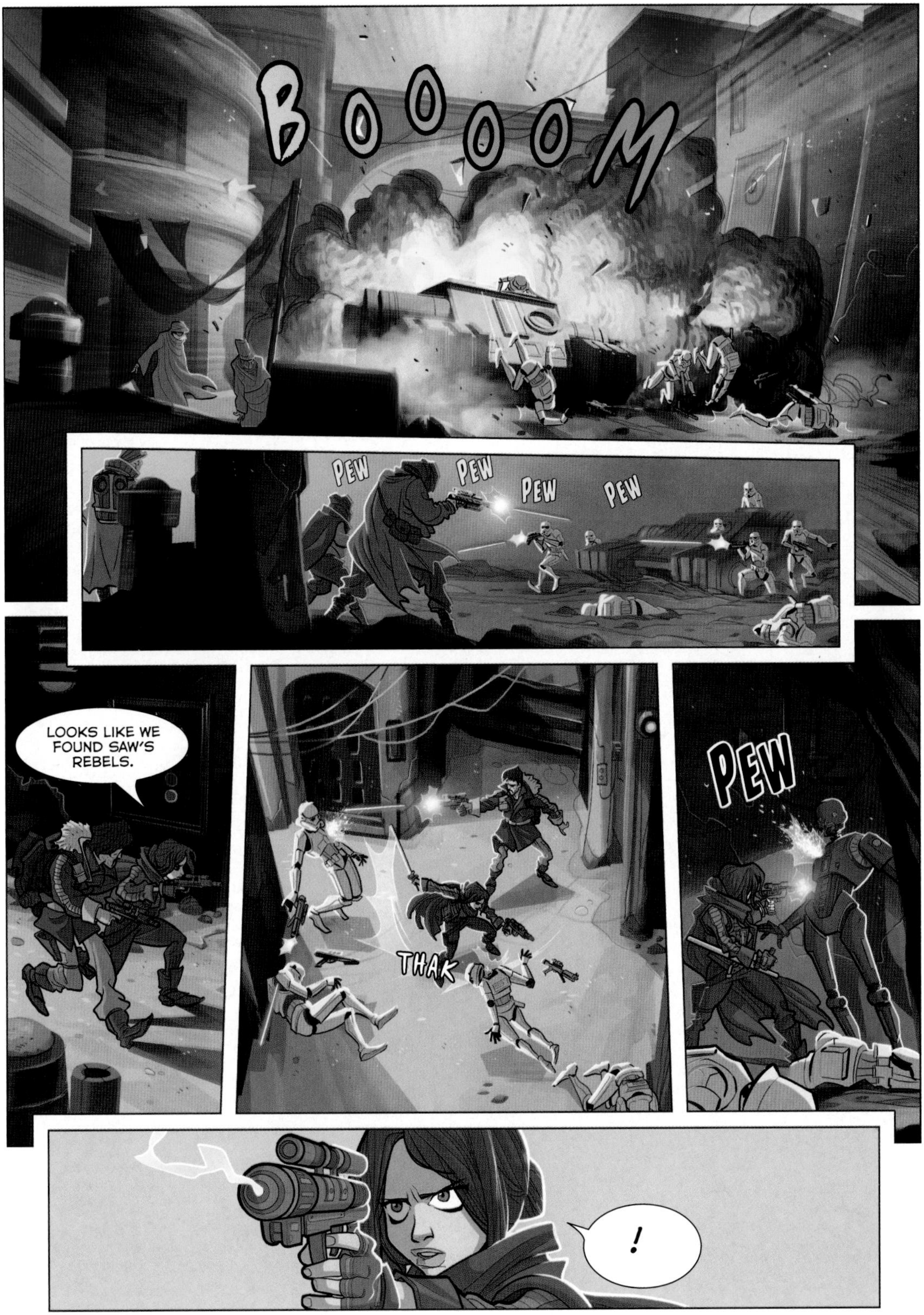
BOOOOM
PEW
PEW
PEW
PEW
LOOKS LIKE WE FOUND SAW'S REBELS.
THAK
PEW
!

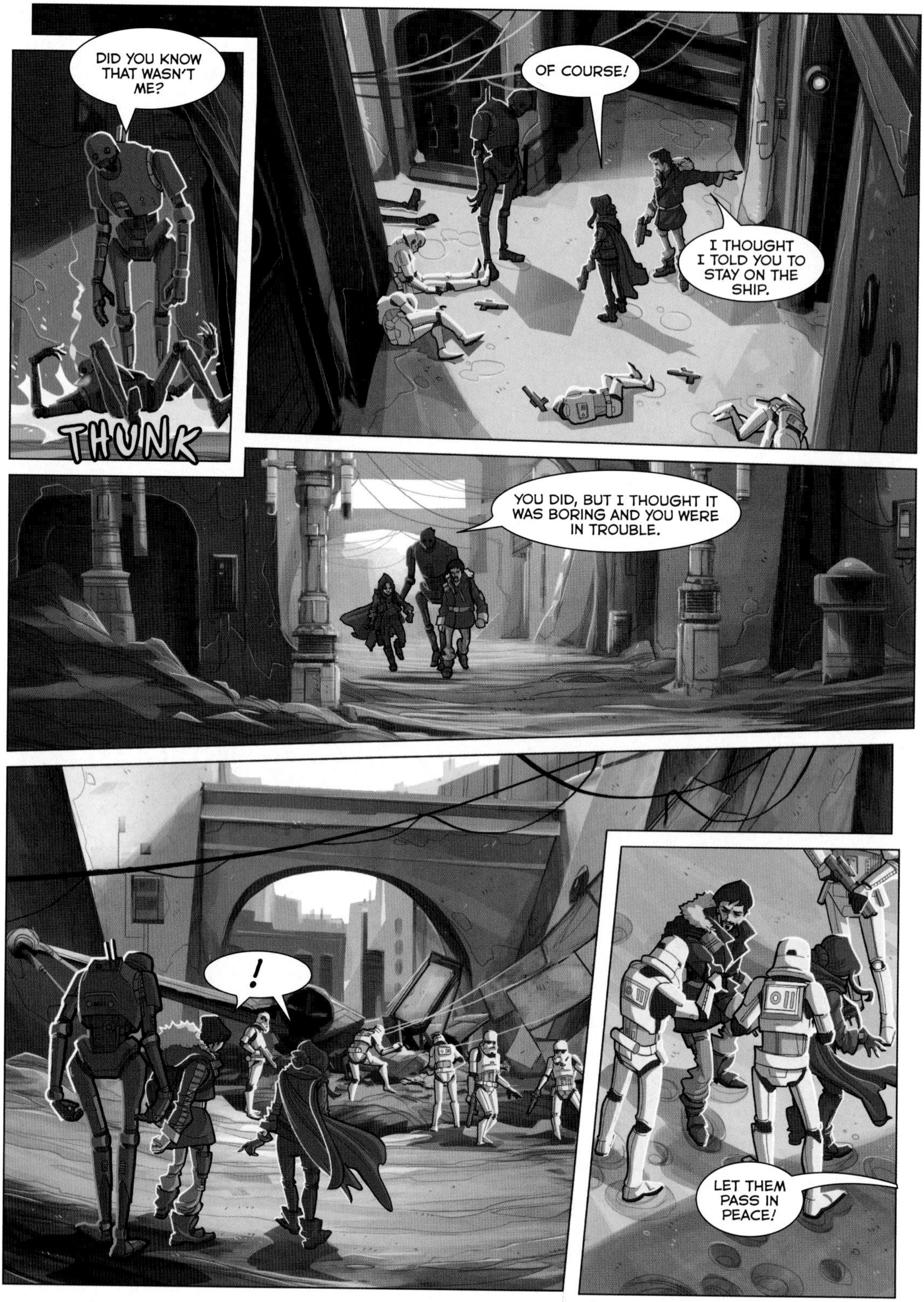
DID YOU KNOW THAT WASN'T ME?
THUNK
OF COURSE!
I THOUGHT I TOLD YOU TO STAY ON THE SHIP.
YOU DID, BUT I THOUGHT IT WAS BORING AND YOU WERE IN TROUBLE.
!
LET THEM PASS IN PEACE!

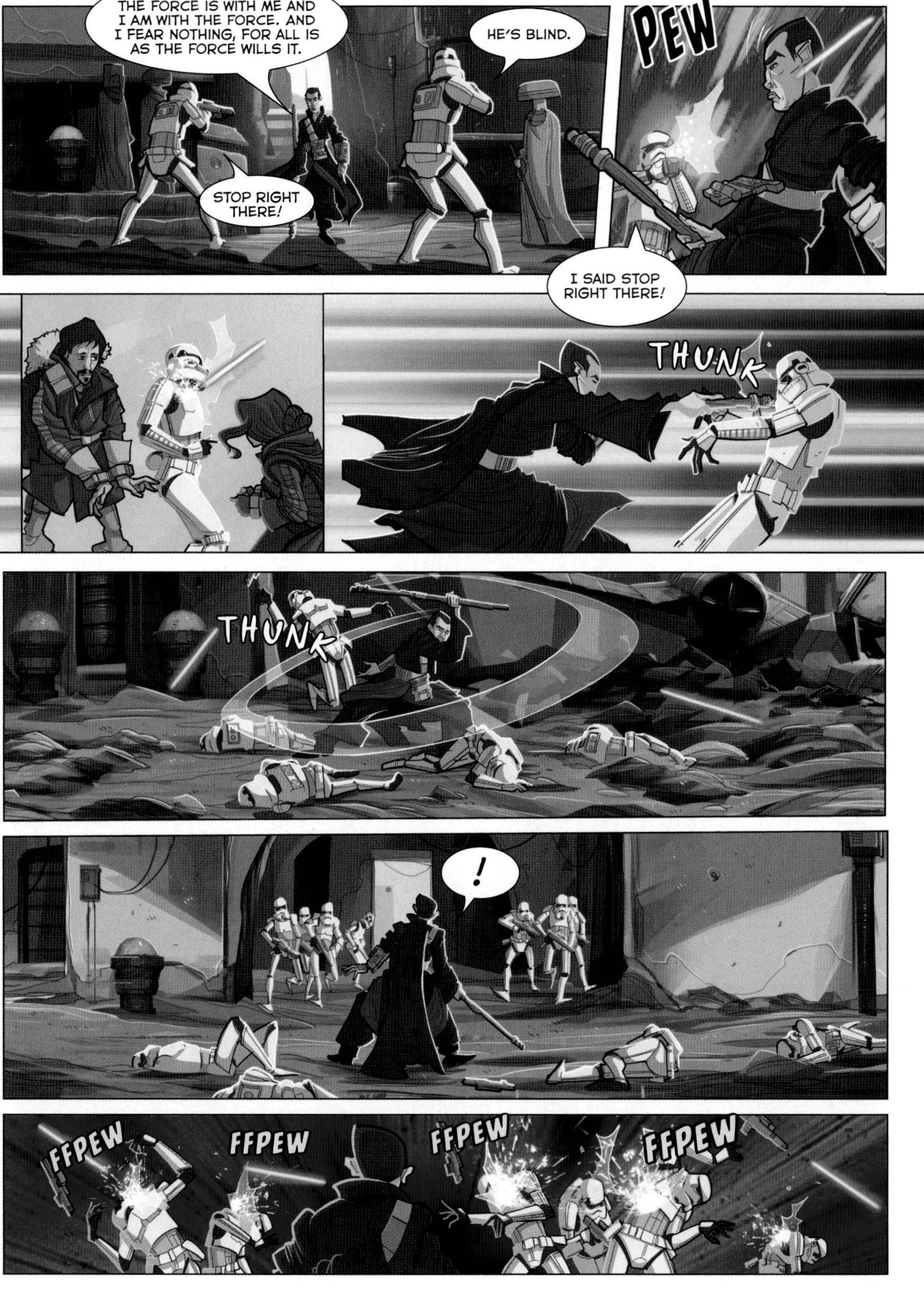
THE FORCE IS WITH ME AND I AM WITH THE FORCE. AND I FEAR NOTHING, FOR ALL IS AS THE FORCE WILLS IT.
STOP RIGHT THERE!
HE'S BLIND.
PEW
I SAID STOP RIGHT THERE!
THUNK
THUNK
!
FFPEW
FFPEW
FFPEW
FFPEW

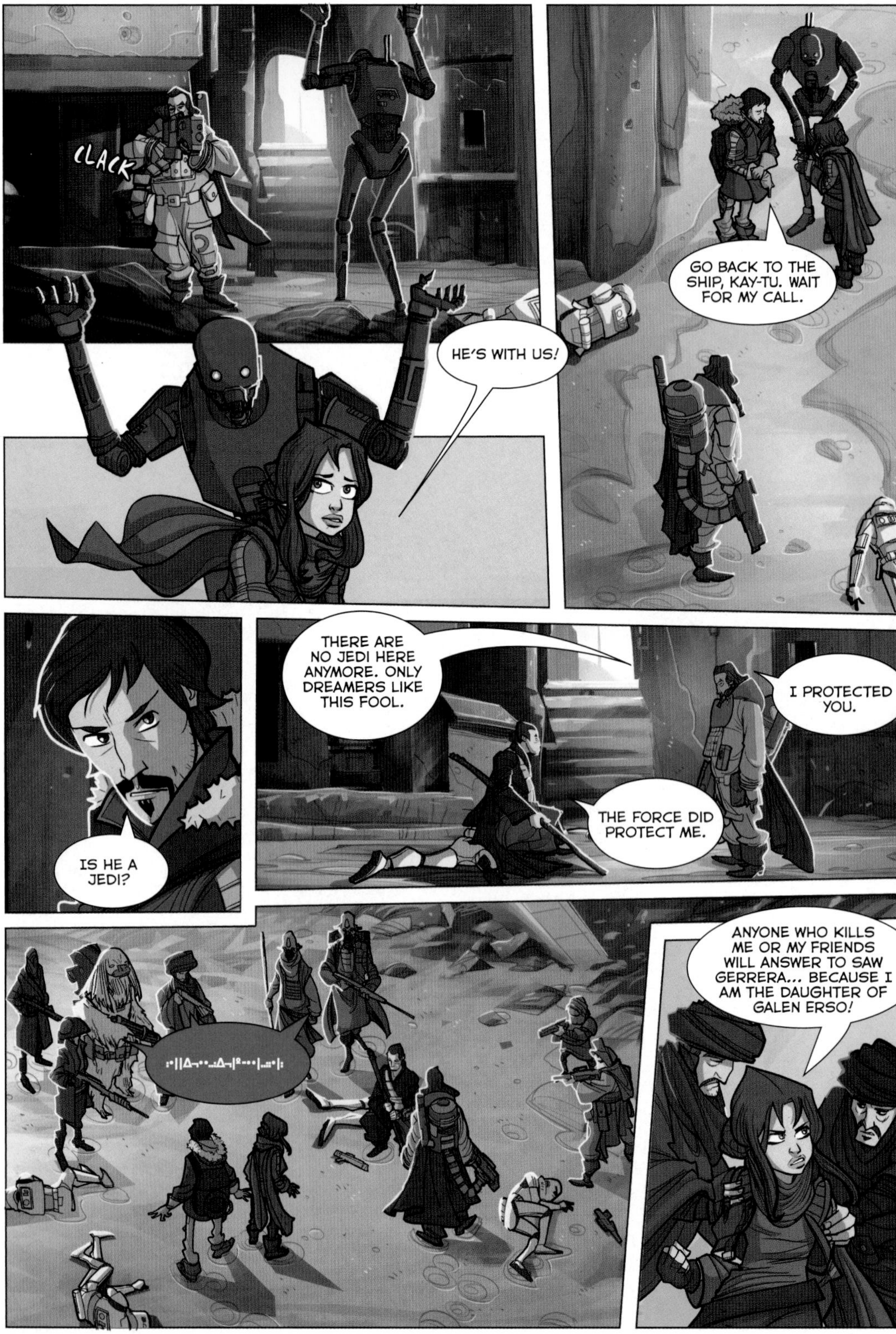
CLACK
HE'S WITH US!
GO BACK TO THE SHIP, KAY-TU. WAIT FOR MY CALL.
IS HE A JEDI?
THERE ARE NO JEDI HERE ANYMORE. ONLY DREAMERS LIKE THIS FOOL.
I PROTECTED YOU.
THE FORCE DID PROTECT ME.
ANYONE WHO KILLS ME OR MY FRIENDS WILL ANSWER TO SAW GERRERA... BECAUSE I AM THE DAUGHTER OF GALEN ERSO!

* HANDS IN THE AIR!

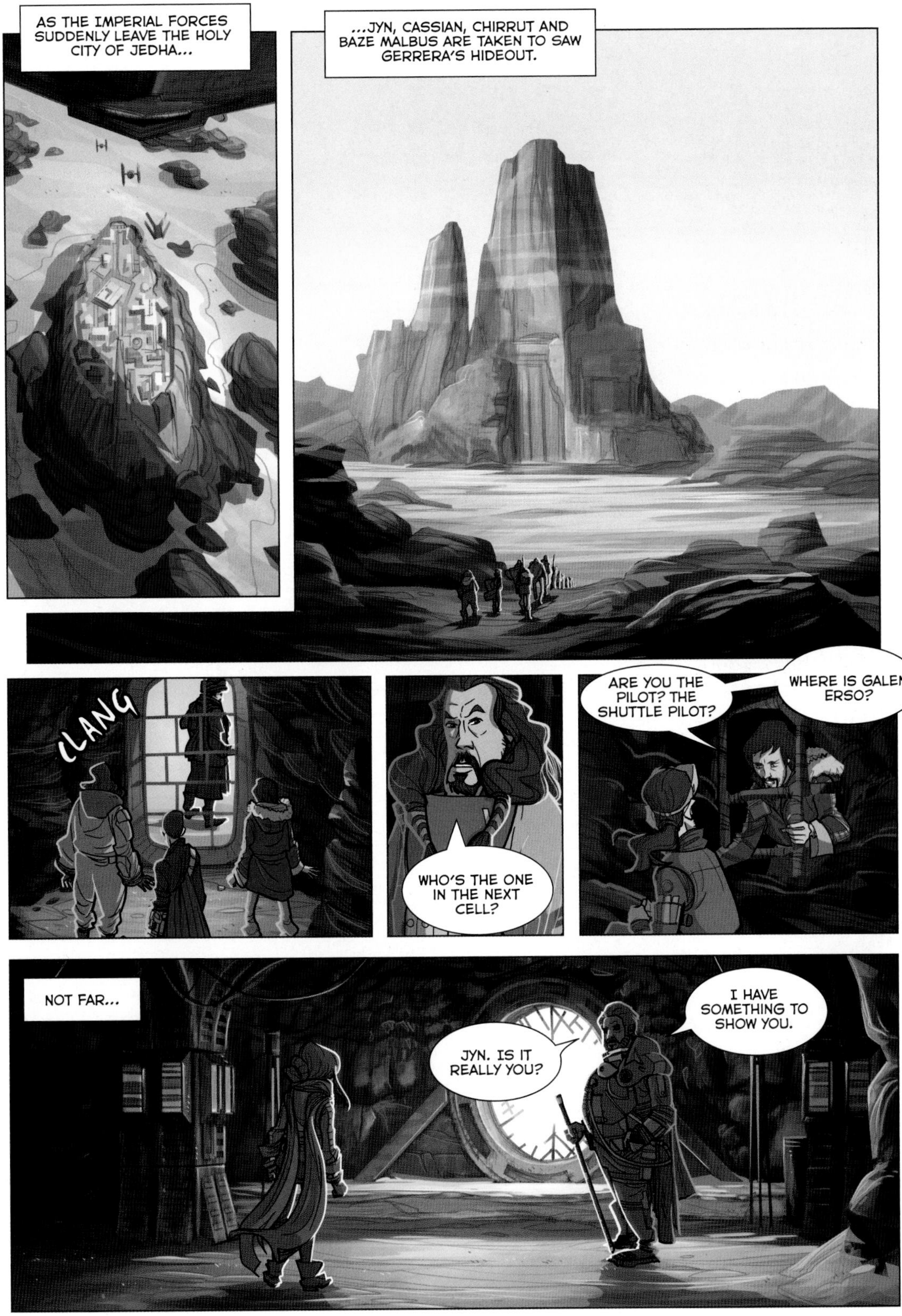
AS THE IMPERIAL FORCES SUDDENLY LEAVE THE HOLY CITY OF JEDHA...
...JYN, CASSIAN, CHIRRUT AND BAZE MALBUS ARE TAKEN TO SAW GERRERA'S HIDEOUT.
CLANG
WHO'S THE ONE IN THE NEXT CELL?
ARE YOU THE PILOT? THE SHUTTLE PILOT?
WHERE IS GALEN ERSO?
NOT FAR...
JYN. IS IT REALLY YOU?
I HAVE SOMETHING TO SHOW YOU.

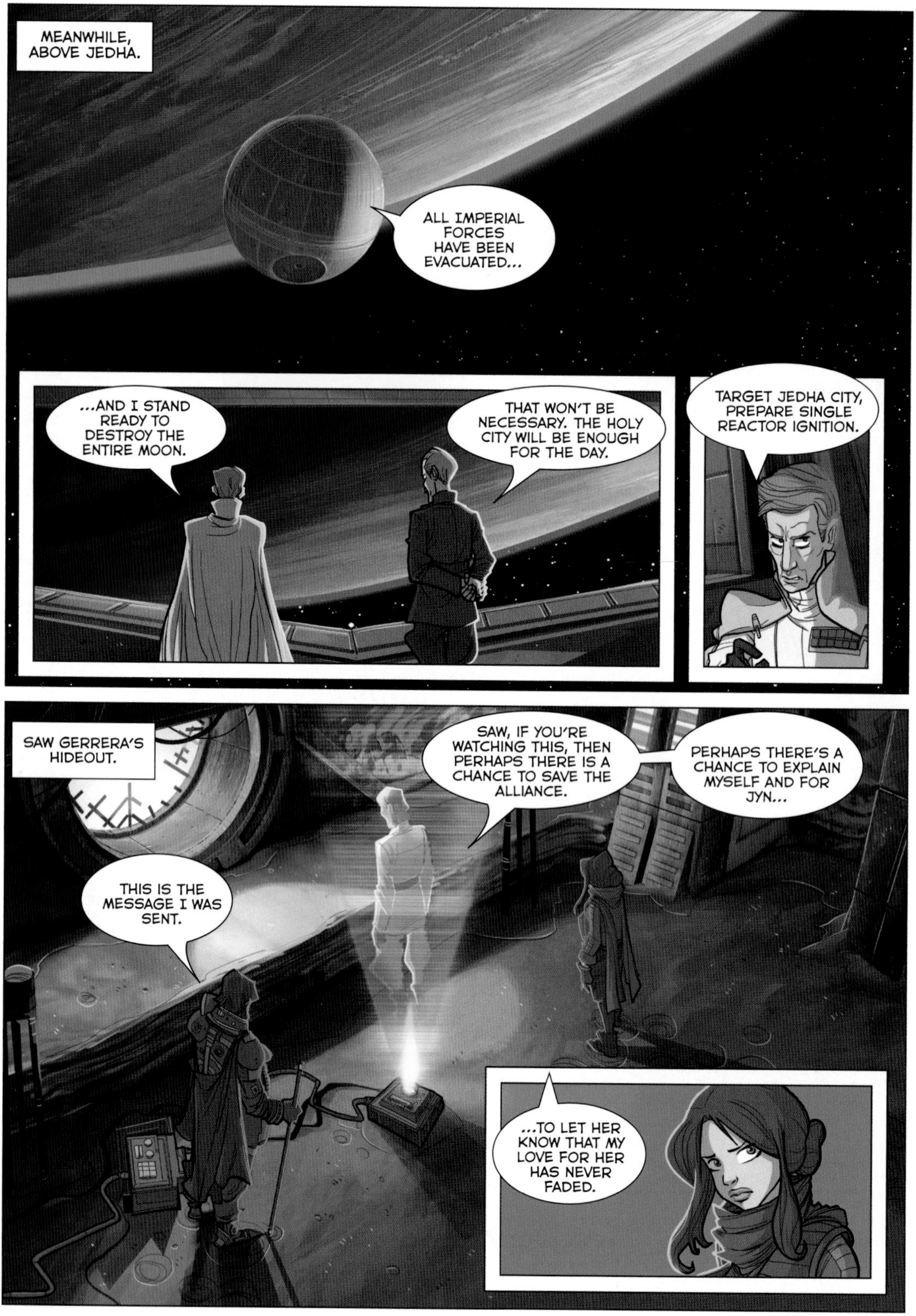
MEANWHILE, ABOVE JEDHA.
ALL IMPERIAL FORCES HAVE BEEN EVACUATED...
...AND I STAND READY TO DESTROY THE ENTIRE MOON.
THAT WON'T BE NECESSARY. THE HOLY CITY WILL BE ENOUGH FOR THE DAY.
TARGET JEDHA CITY, PREPARE SINGLE REACTOR IGNITION.
SAW GERRERA'S HIDEOUT.
THIS IS THE MESSAGE I WAS SENT.
SAW, IF YOU'RE WATCHING THIS, THEN PERHAPS THERE IS A CHANCE TO SAVE THE ALLIANCE.
PERHAPS THERE'S A CHANCE TO EXPLAIN MYSELF AND FOR JYN...
...TO LET HER KNOW THAT MY LOVE FOR HER HAS NEVER FADED.

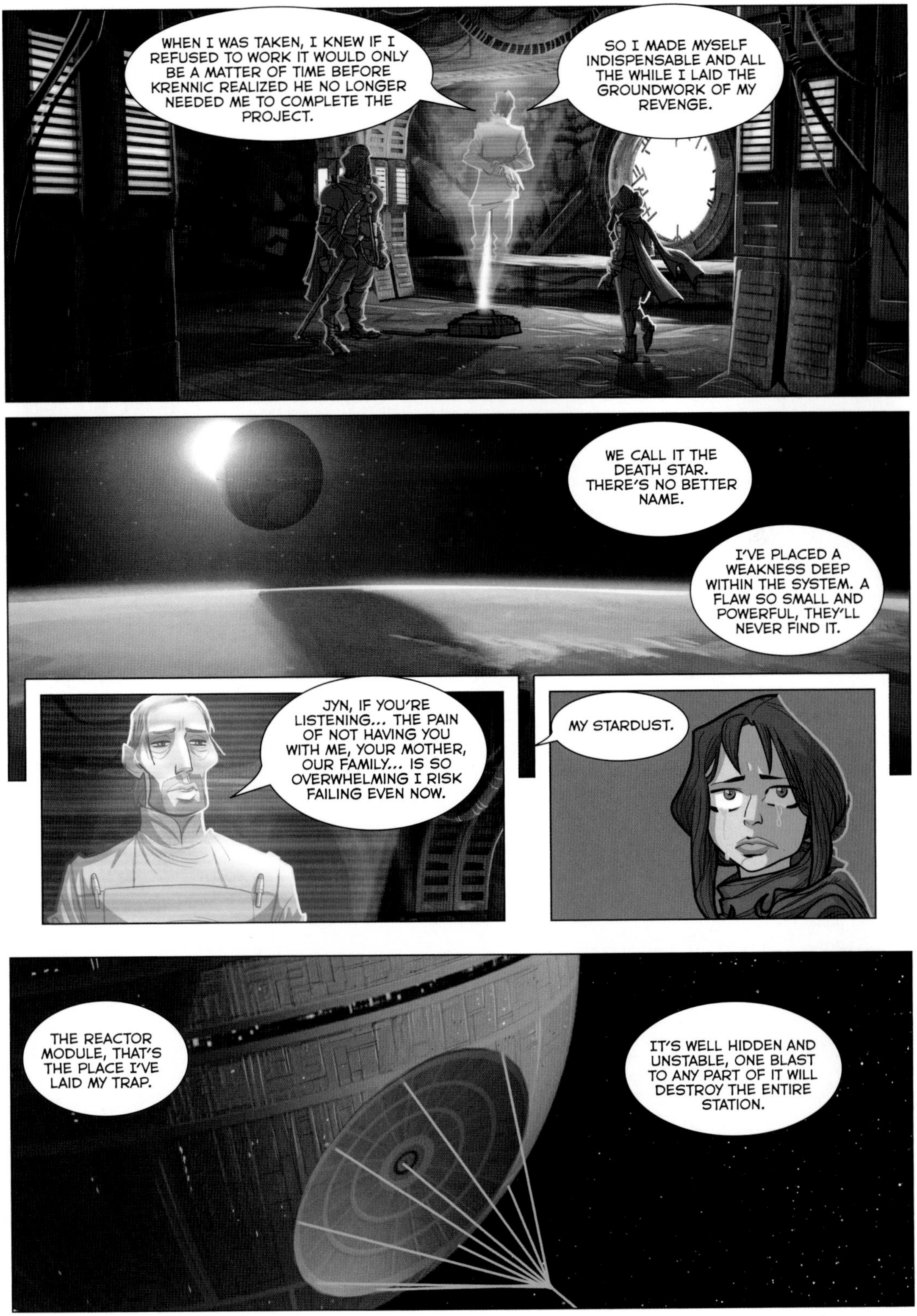
WHEN I WAS TAKEN, I KNEW IF I REFUSED TO WORK IT WOULD ONLY BE A MATTER OF TIME BEFORE KRENNIC REALIZED HE NO LONGER NEEDED ME TO COMPLETE THE PROJECT.
SO I MADE MYSELF INDISPENSABLE AND ALL THE WHILE I LAID THE GROUNDWORK OF MY REVENGE.
WE CALL IT THE DEATH STAR. THERE'S NO BETTER NAME.
I'VE PLACED A WEAKNESS DEEP WITHIN THE SYSTEM. A FLAW SO SMALL AND POWERFUL, THEY'LL NEVER FIND IT.
JYN, IF YOU'RE LISTENING... THE PAIN OF NOT HAVING YOU WITH ME, YOUR MOTHER, OUR FAMILY... IS SO OVERWHELMING I RISK FAILING EVEN NOW.
MY STARDUST.
THE REACTOR MODULE, THAT'S THE PLACE I'VE LAID MY TRAP.
IT'S WELL HIDDEN AND UNSTABLE, ONE BLAST TO ANY PART OF IT WILL DESTROY THE ENTIRE STATION.

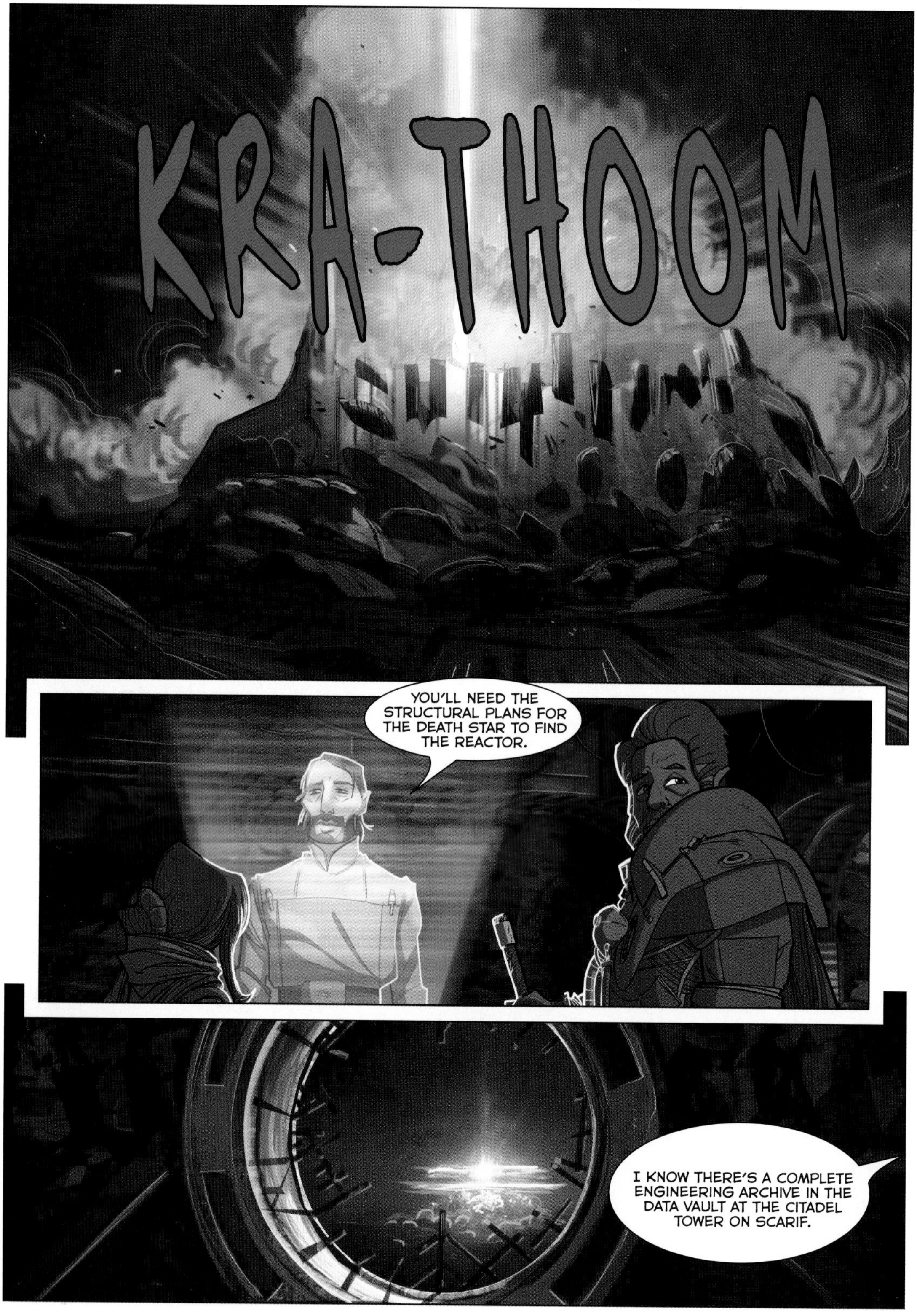
KRA-THOOM
YOU'LL NEED THE STRUCTURAL PLANS FOR THE DEATH STAR TO FIND THE REACTOR.
I KNOW THERE'S A COMPLETE ENGINEERING ARCHIVE IN THE DATA VAULT AT THE CITADEL TOWER ON SCARIF.

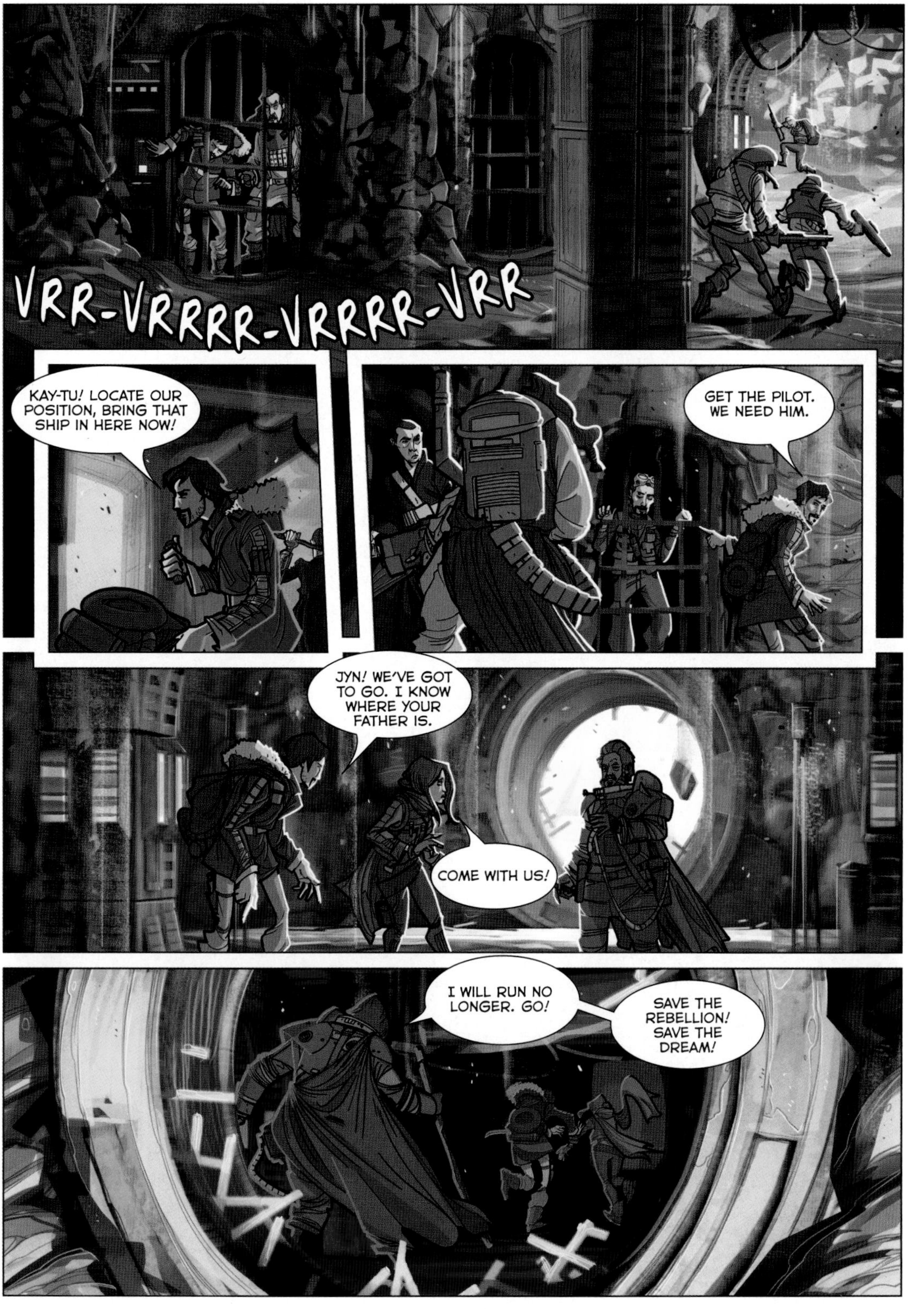
VRR-VRRRR-VRRRR-VRR
KAY-TU! LOCATE OUR POSITION, BRING THAT SHIP IN HERE NOW!
GET THE PILOT. WE NEED HIM.
JYN! WE'VE GOT TO GO. I KNOW WHERE YOUR FATHER IS.
COME WITH US!
I WILL RUN NO LONGER. GO!
SAVE THE REBELLION! SAVE THE DREAM!

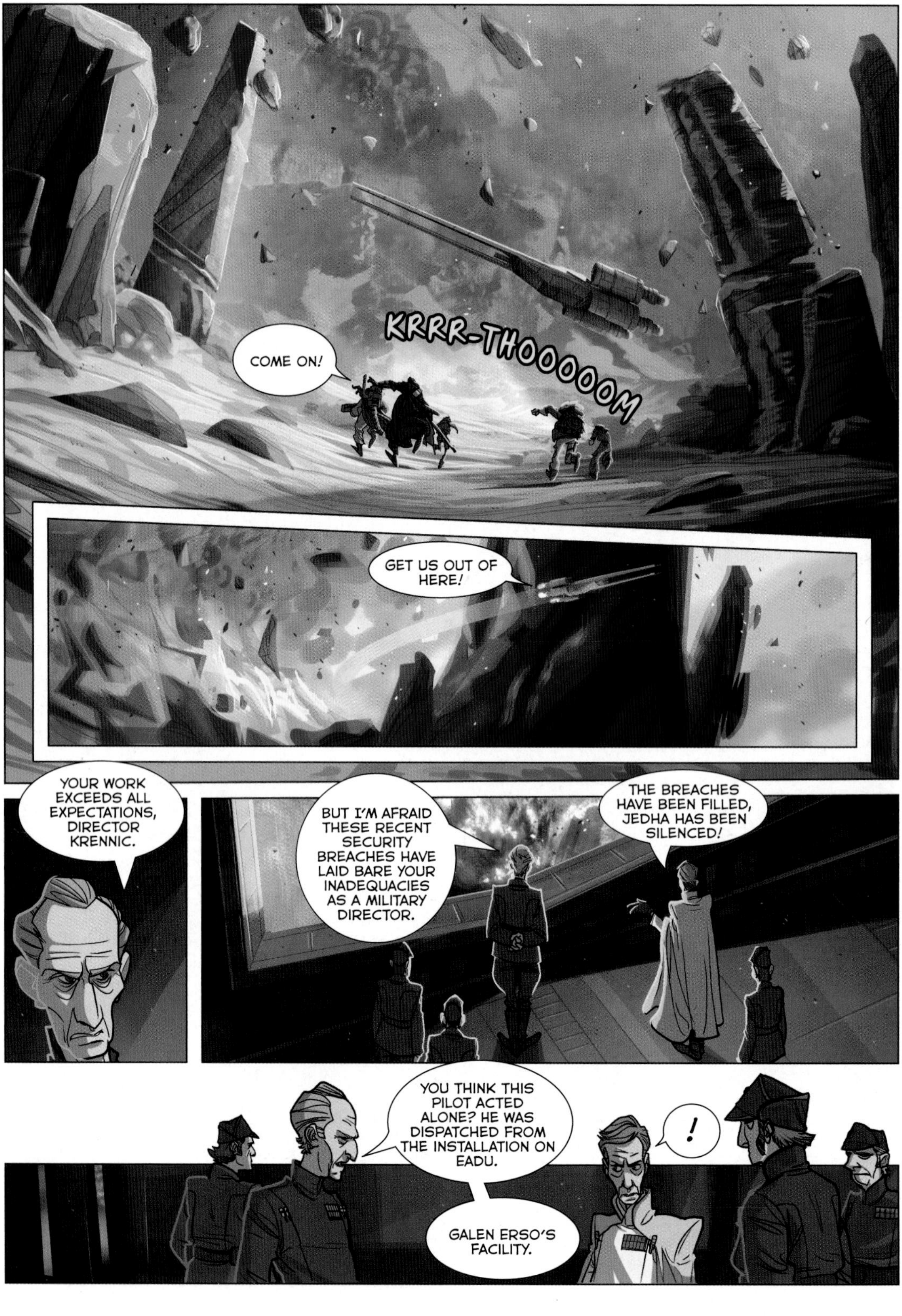
COME ON!
KRRR-THOOOOOM
GET US OUT OF HERE!
YOUR WORK EXCEEDS ALL EXPECTATIONS, DIRECTOR KRENNIC.
BUT I'M AFRAID THESE RECENT SECURITY BREACHES HAVE LAID BARE YOUR INADEQUACIES AS A MILITARY DIRECTOR.
THE BREACHES HAVE BEEN FILLED, JEDHA HAS BEEN SILENCED!
YOU THINK THIS PILOT ACTED ALONE? HE WAS DISPATCHED FROM THE INSTALLATION ON EADU.
!
GALEN ERSO'S FACILITY.

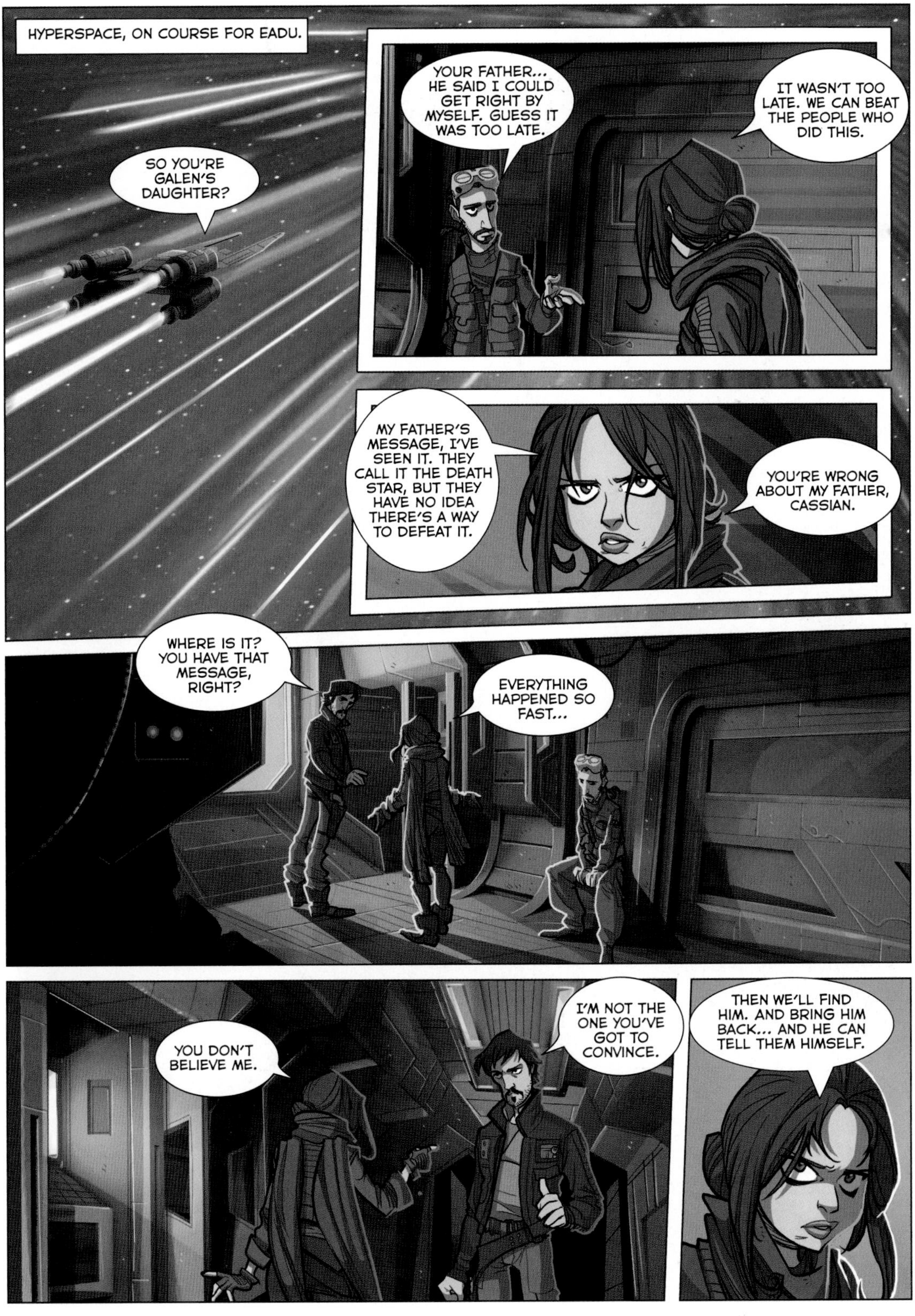

HYPERSPACE, ON COURSE FOR EADU.
SO YOU'RE GALEN'S DAUGHTER?
YOUR FATHER... HE SAID I COULD GET RIGHT BY MYSELF. GUESS IT WAS TOO LATE.
IT WASN'T TOO LATE. WE CAN BEAT THE PEOPLE WHO DID THIS.
MY FATHER'S MESSAGE, I'VE SEEN IT. THEY CALL IT THE DEATH STAR, BUT THEY HAVE NO IDEA THERE'S A WAY TO DEFEAT IT.
YOU'RE WRONG ABOUT MY FATHER, CASSIAN.
WHERE IS IT? YOU HAVE THAT MESSAGE, RIGHT?
EVERYTHING HAPPENED SO FAST...
YOU DON'T BELIEVE ME.
I'M NOT THE ONE YOU'VE GOT TO CONVINCE.
THEN WE'LL FIND HIM. AND BRING HIM BACK... AND HE CAN TELL THEM HIMSELF.

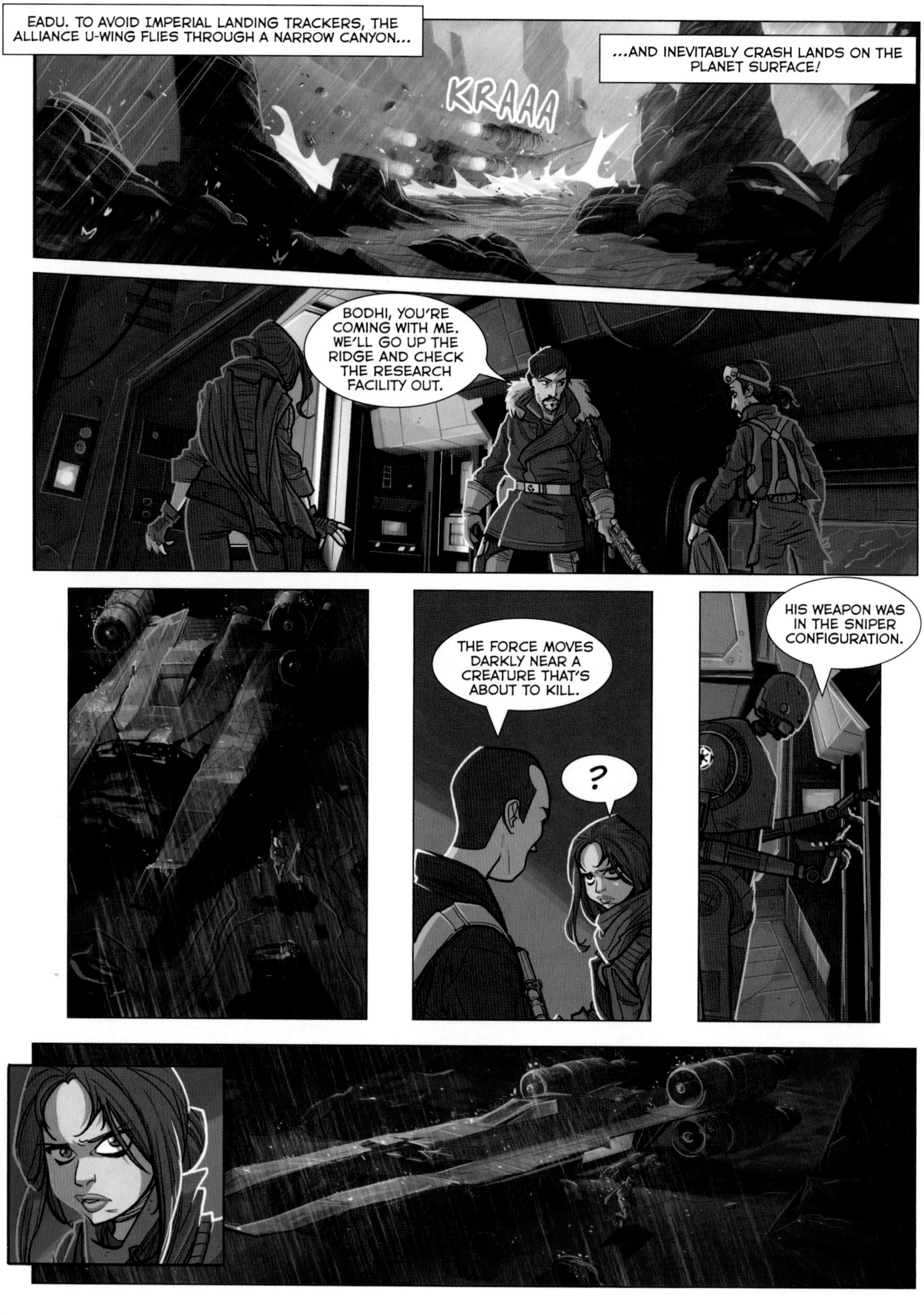
EADU. TO AVOID IMPERIAL LANDING TRACKERS, THE ALLIANCE U-WING FLIES THROUGH A NARROW CANYON...
...AND INEVITABLY CRASH LANDS ON THE PLANET SURFACE!
KRAAA
BODHI, YOU'RE COMING WITH ME. WE'LL GO UP THE RIDGE AND CHECK THE RESEARCH FACILITY OUT.
THE FORCE MOVES DARKLY NEAR A CREATURE THAT'S ABOUT TO KILL.
?
HIS WEAPON WAS IN THE SNIPER CONFIGURATION.

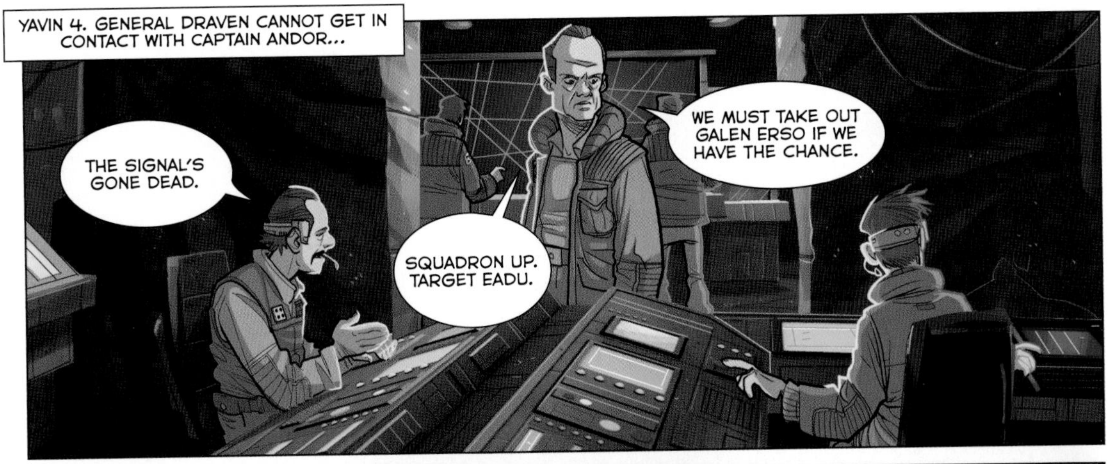
YAVIN 4. GENERAL DRAVEN CANNOT GET IN CONTACT WITH CAPTAIN ANDOR...
THE SIGNAL'S GONE DEAD.
SQUADRON UP. TARGET EADU.
WE MUST TAKE OUT GALEN ERSO IF WE HAVE THE CHANCE.

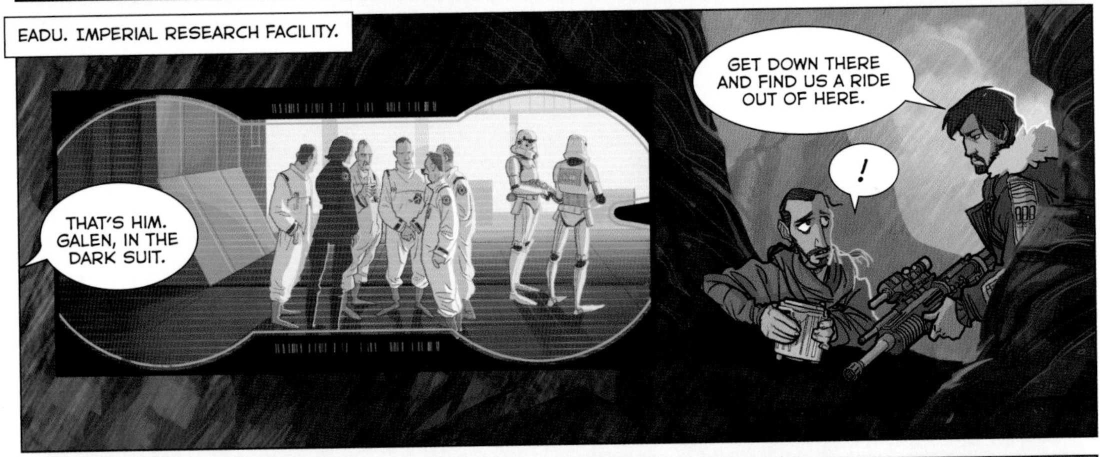
EADU. IMPERIAL RESEARCH FACILITY.
THAT'S HIM. GALEN, IN THE DARK SUIT.
GET DOWN THERE AND FIND US A RIDE OUT OF HERE.
!

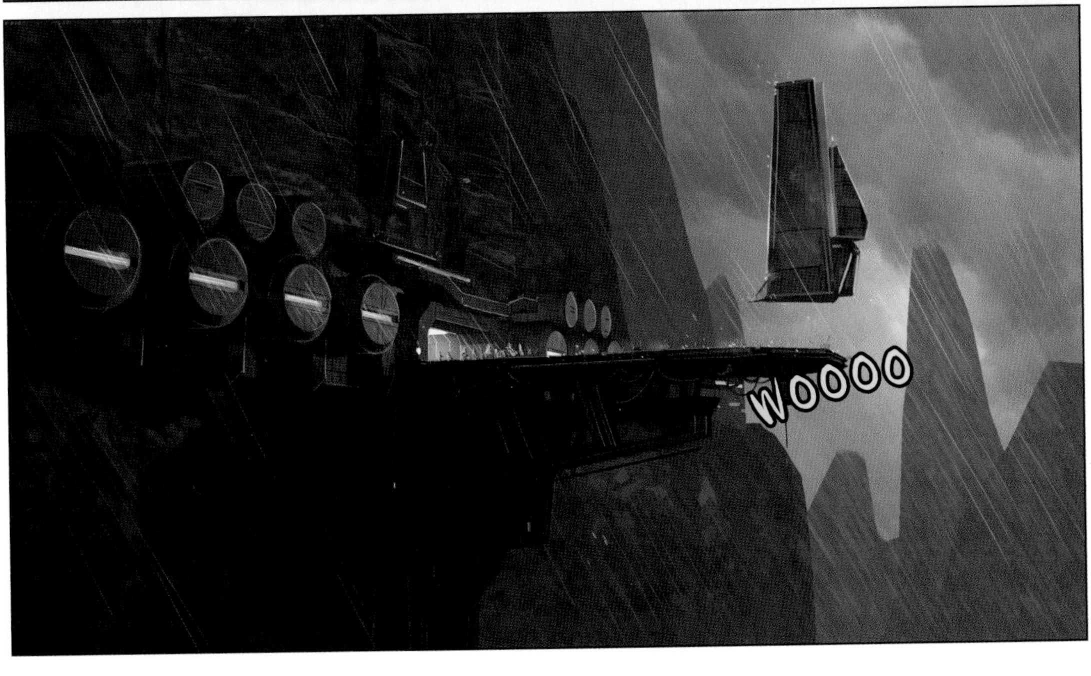
WOOOO

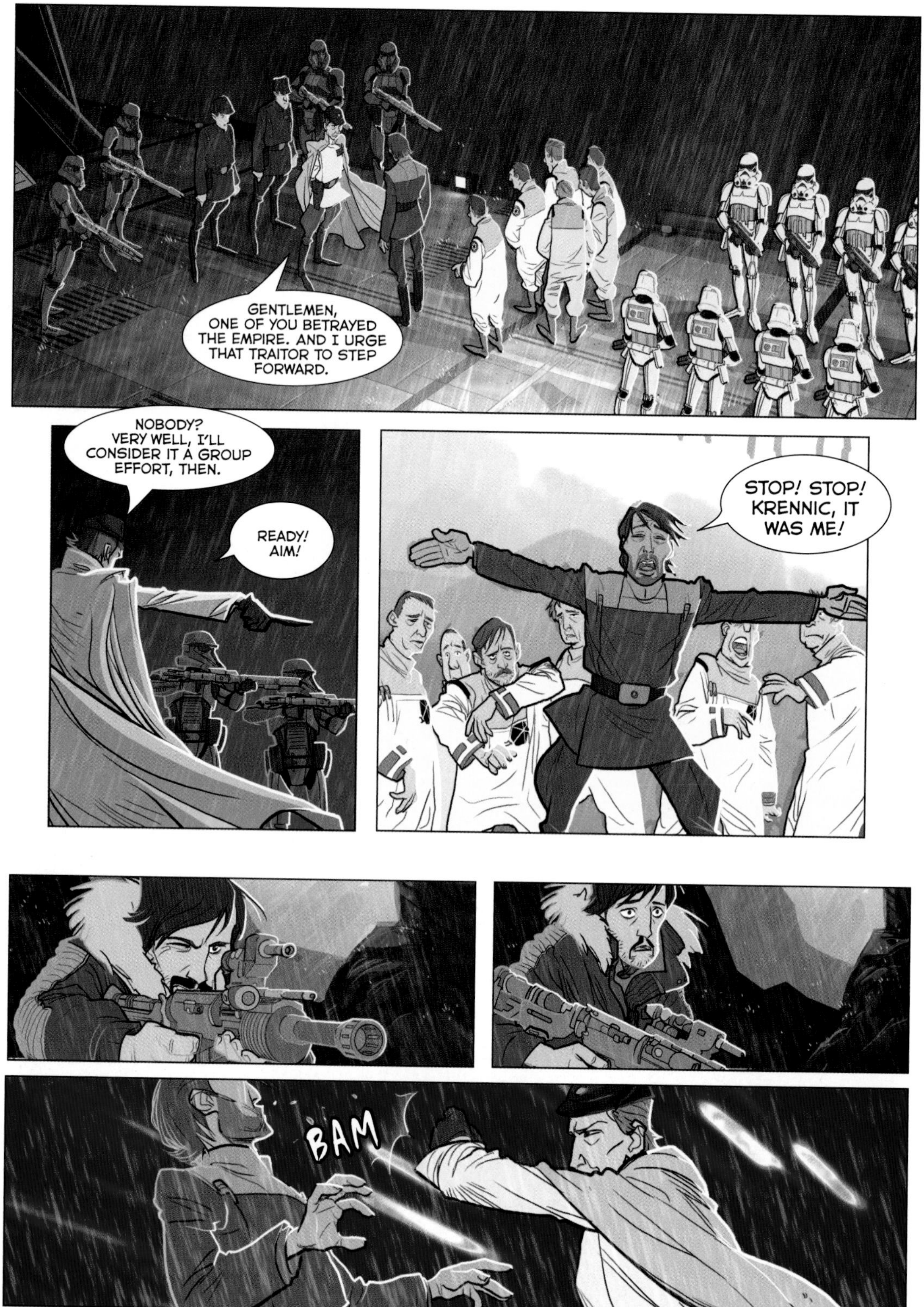
GENTLEMEN, ONE OF YOU BETRAYED THE EMPIRE. AND I URGE THAT TRAITOR TO STEP FORWARD.
NOBODY? VERY WELL, I'LL CONSIDER IT A GROUP EFFORT, THEN.
READY! AIM!
STOP! STOP! KRENNIC, IT WAS ME!
BAM

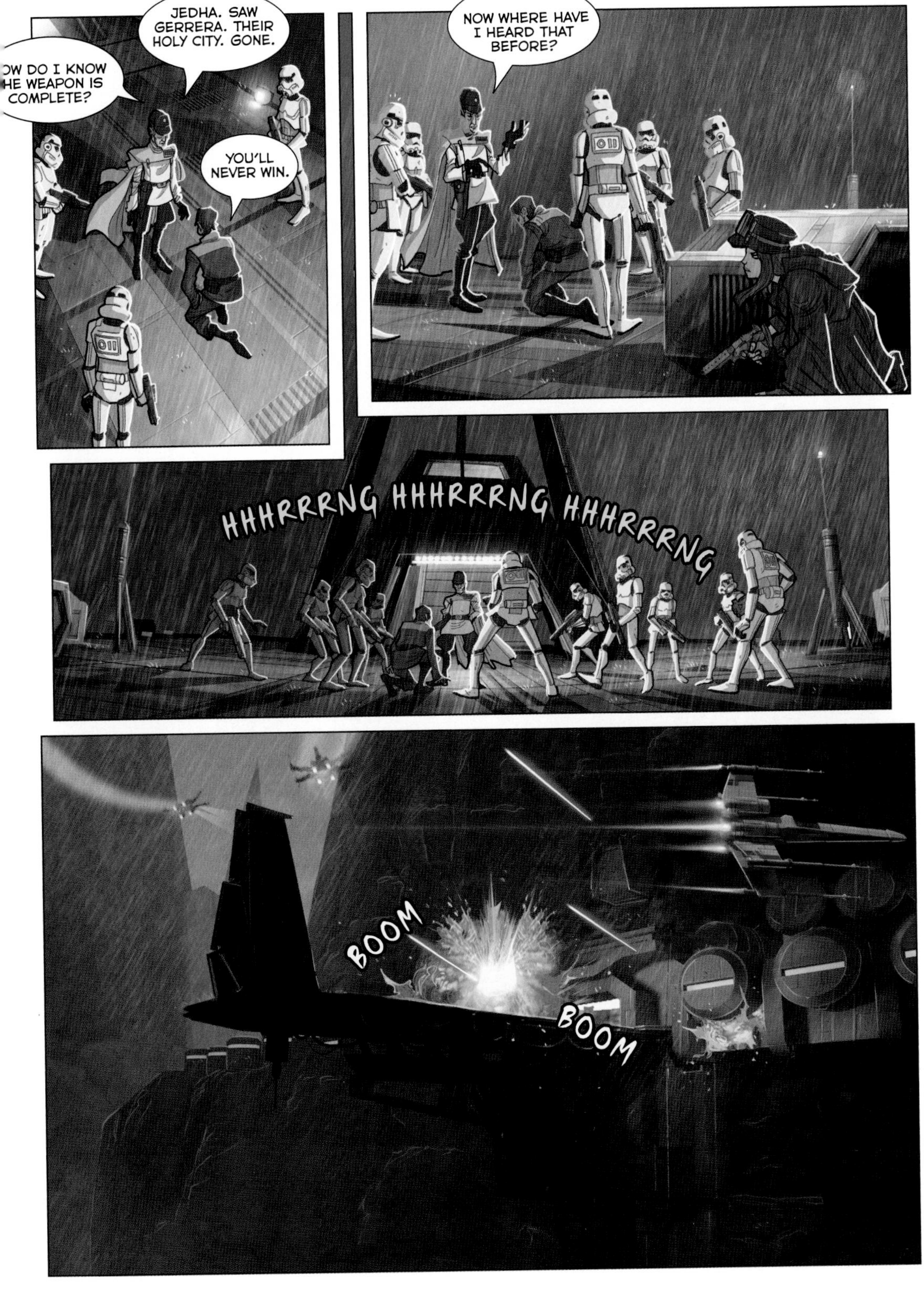
OW DO I KNOW HE WEAPON IS COMPLETE?
JEDHA. SAW GERRERA. THEIR HOLY CITY. GONE.
YOU'LL NEVER WIN.
NOW WHERE HAVE I HEARD THAT BEFORE?
HHHRRRNG HHHRRRNG HHHRRRNG
BOOM
BOOM

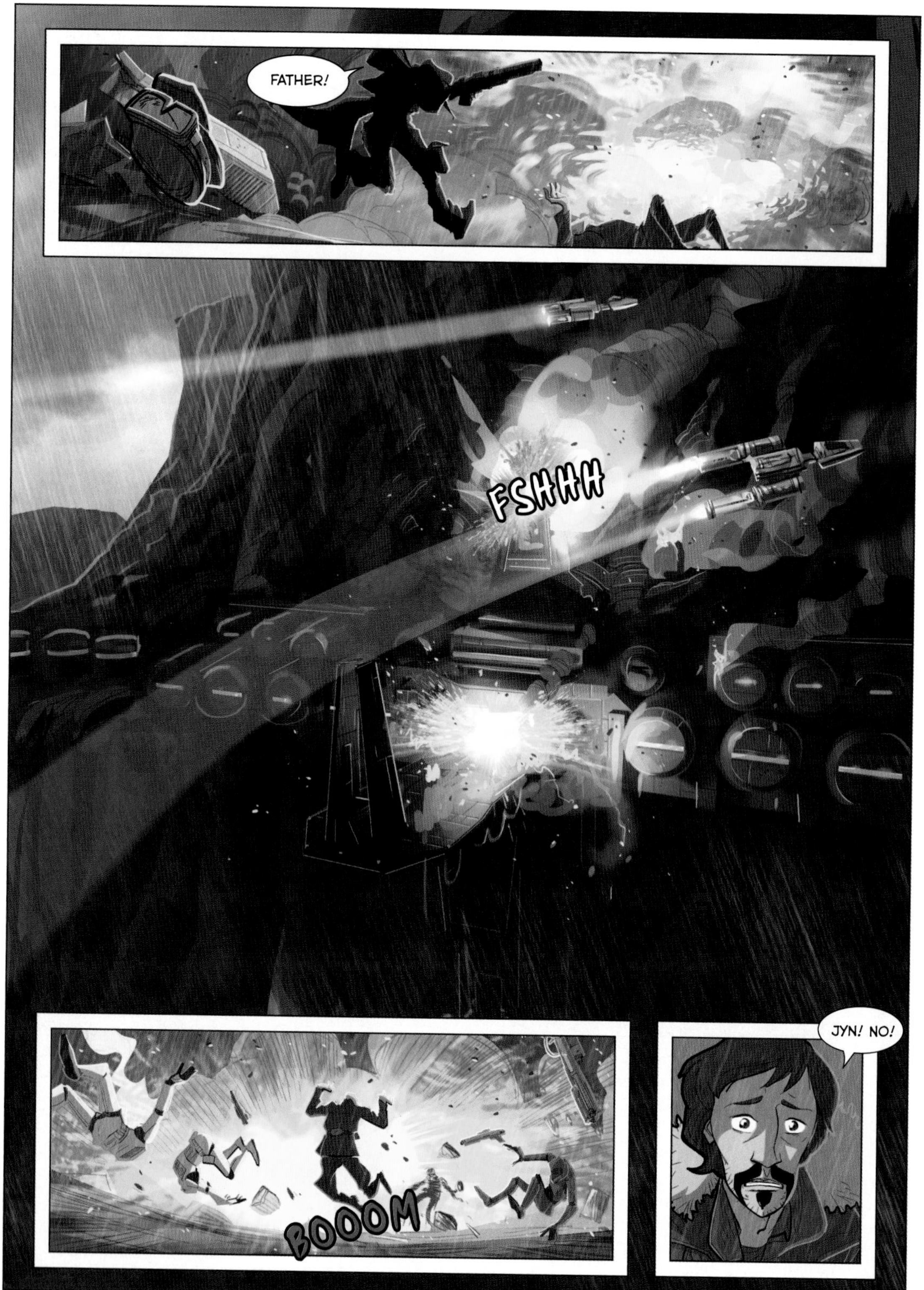

FATHER!
FSHHH
BOOOM
JYN! NO!

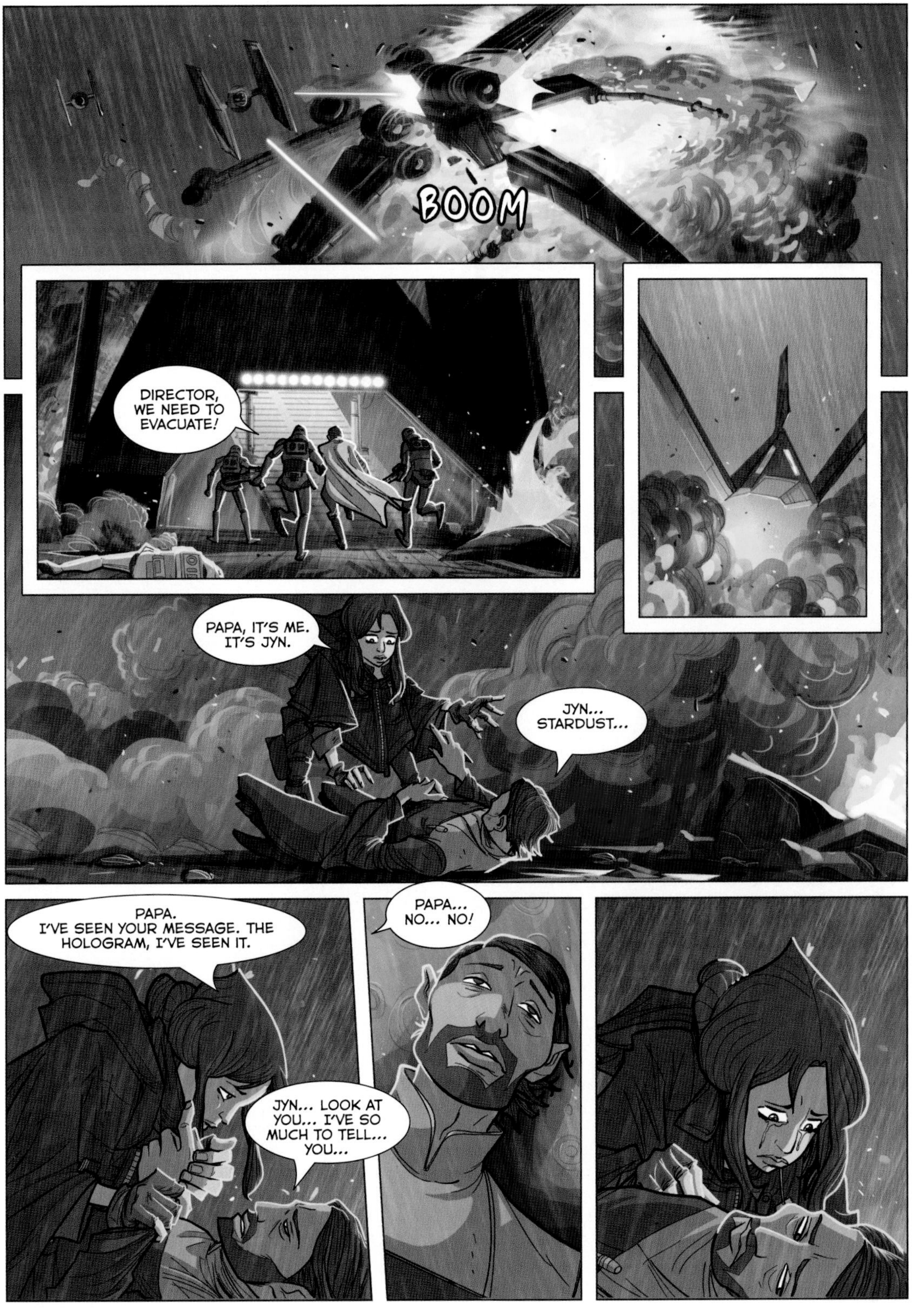
BOOM
DIRECTOR, WE NEED TO EVACUATE!
PAPA, IT'S ME. IT'S JYN.
JYN... STARDUST...
PAPA. I'VE SEEN YOUR MESSAGE. THE HOLOGRAM, I'VE SEEN IT.
JYN... LOOK AT YOU... I'VE SO MUCH TO TELL... YOU...
PAPA... NO... NO!

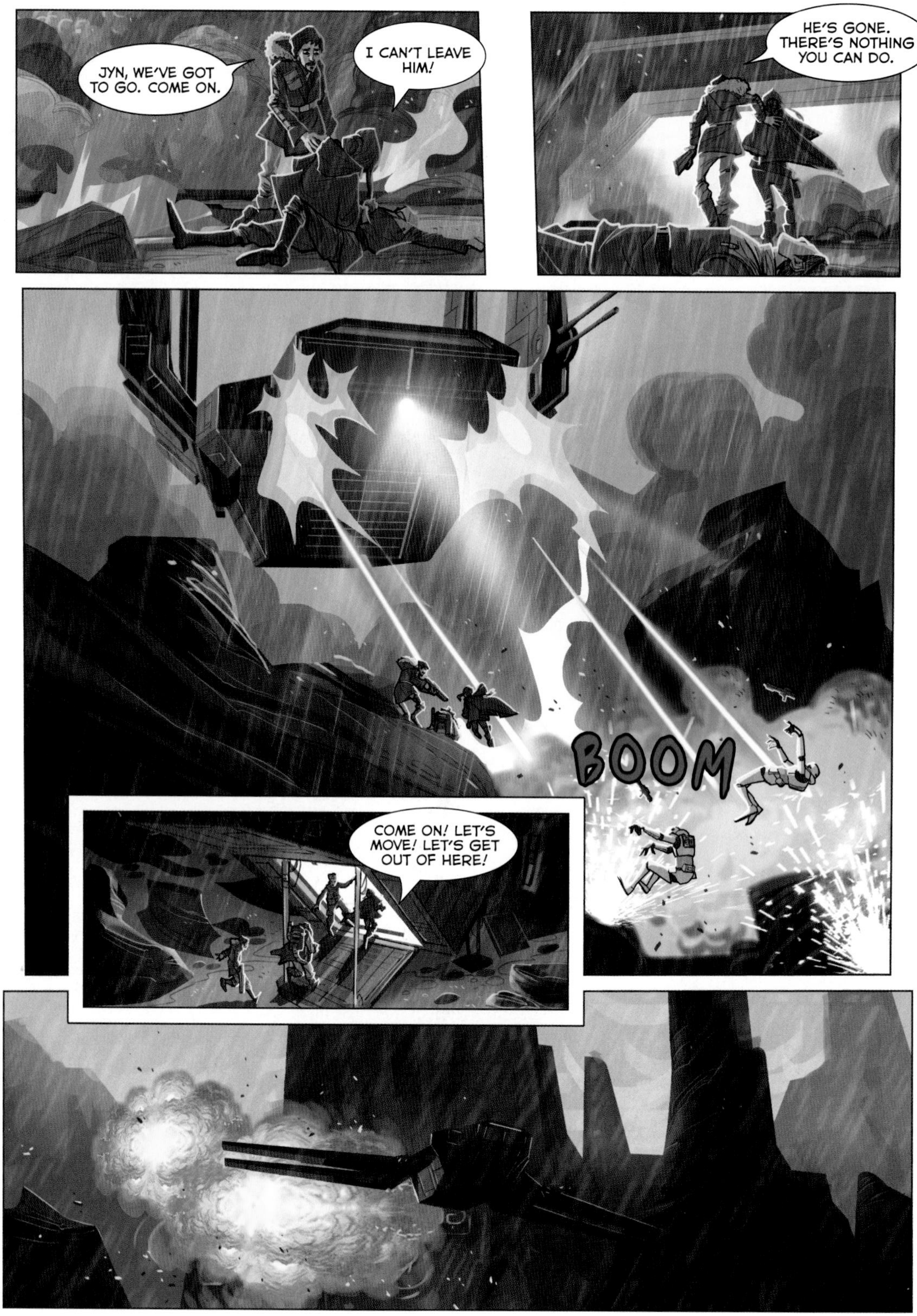
JYN, WE'VE GOT TO GO. COME ON.
I CAN'T LEAVE HIM!
HE'S GONE. THERE'S NOTHING YOU CAN DO.
BOOM
COME ON! LET'S MOVE! LET'S GET OUT OF HERE!

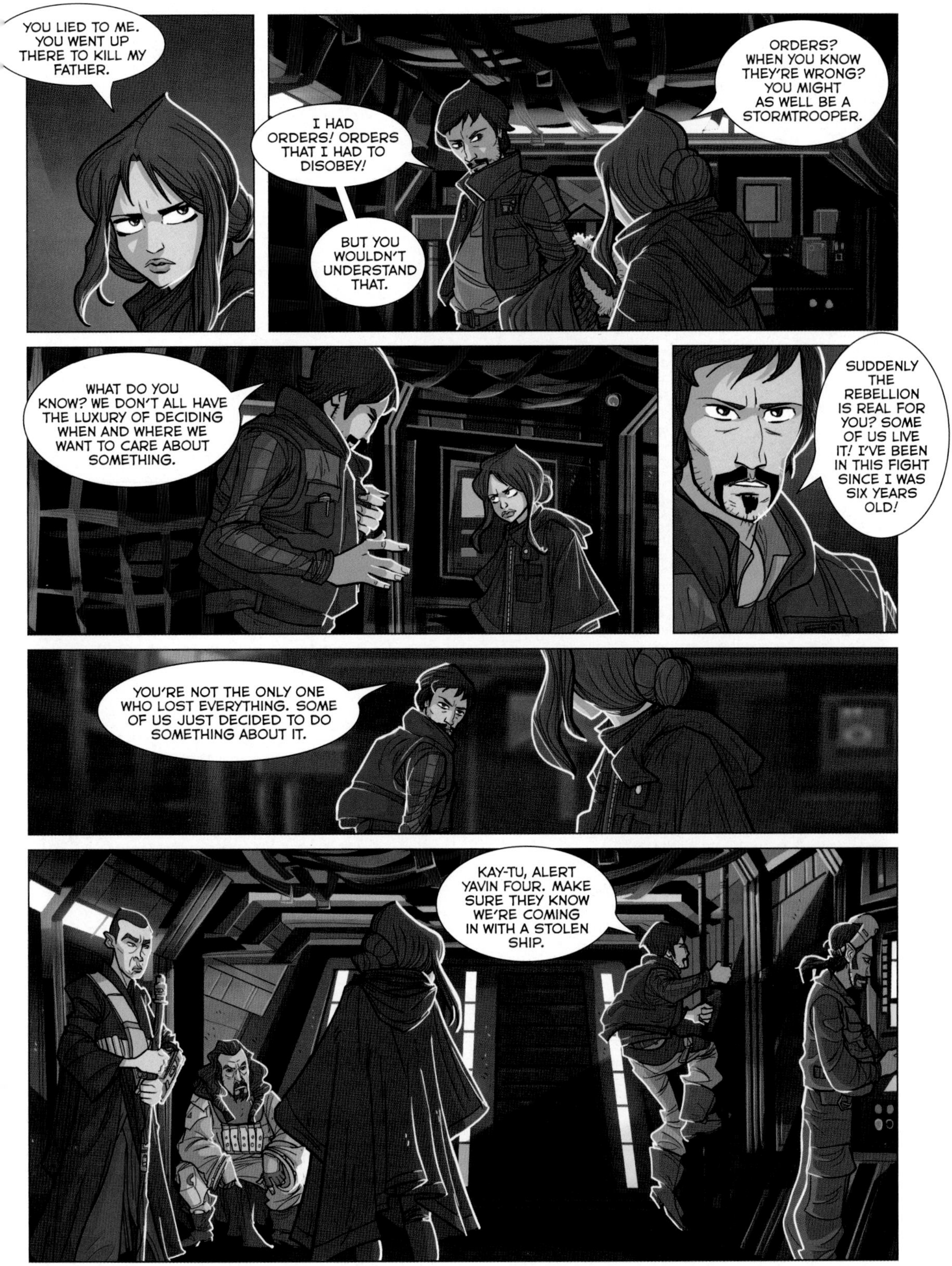
YOU LIED TO ME. YOU WENT UP THERE TO KILL MY FATHER.
I HAD ORDERS! ORDERS THAT I HAD TO DISOBEY!
BUT YOU WOULDN'T UNDERSTAND THAT.
ORDERS? WHEN YOU KNOW THEY'RE WRONG? YOU MIGHT AS WELL BE A STORMTROOPER.
WHAT DO YOU KNOW? WE DON'T ALL HAVE THE LUXURY OF DECIDING WHEN AND WHERE WE WANT TO CARE ABOUT SOMETHING.
SUDDENLY THE REBELLION IS REAL FOR YOU? SOME OF US LIVE IT! I'VE BEEN IN THIS FIGHT SINCE I WAS SIX YEARS OLD!
YOU'RE NOT THE ONLY ONE WHO LOST EVERYTHING. SOME OF US JUST DECIDED TO DO SOMETHING ABOUT IT.
KAY-TU, ALERT YAVIN FOUR. MAKE SURE THEY KNOW WE'RE COMING IN WITH A STOLEN SHIP.

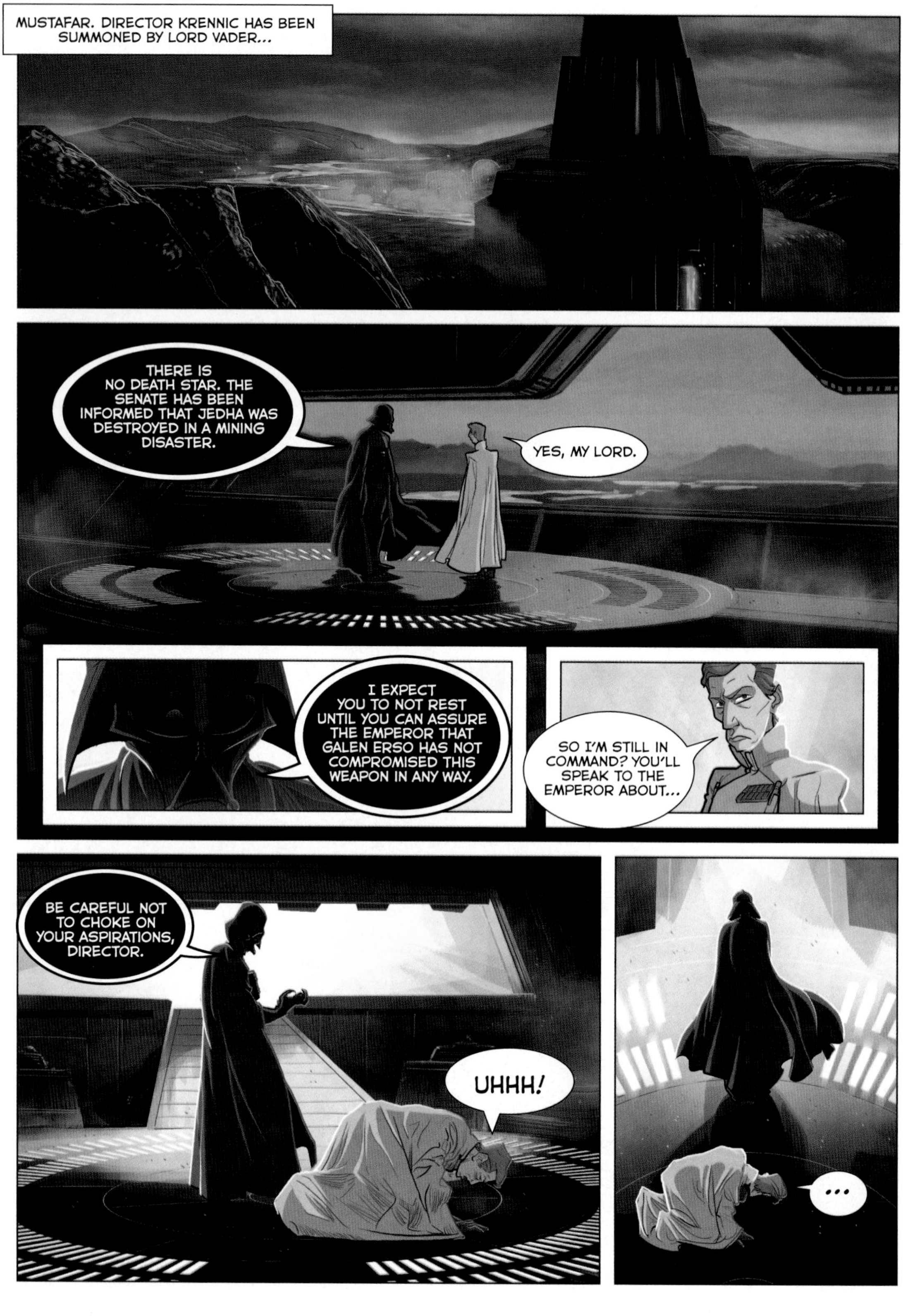
MUSTAFAR. DIRECTOR KRENNIC HAS BEEN SUMMONED BY LORD VADER...
THERE IS NO DEATH STAR. THE SENATE HAS BEEN INFORMED THAT JEDHA WAS DESTROYED IN A MINING DISASTER.
YES, MY LORD.
I EXPECT YOU TO NOT REST UNTIL YOU CAN ASSURE THE EMPEROR THAT GALEN ERSO HAS NOT COMPROMISED THIS WEAPON IN ANY WAY.
SO I'M STILL IN COMMAND? YOU'LL SPEAK TO THE EMPEROR ABOUT...
BE CAREFUL NOT TO CHOKE ON YOUR ASPIRATIONS, DIRECTOR.
UHHH!
...

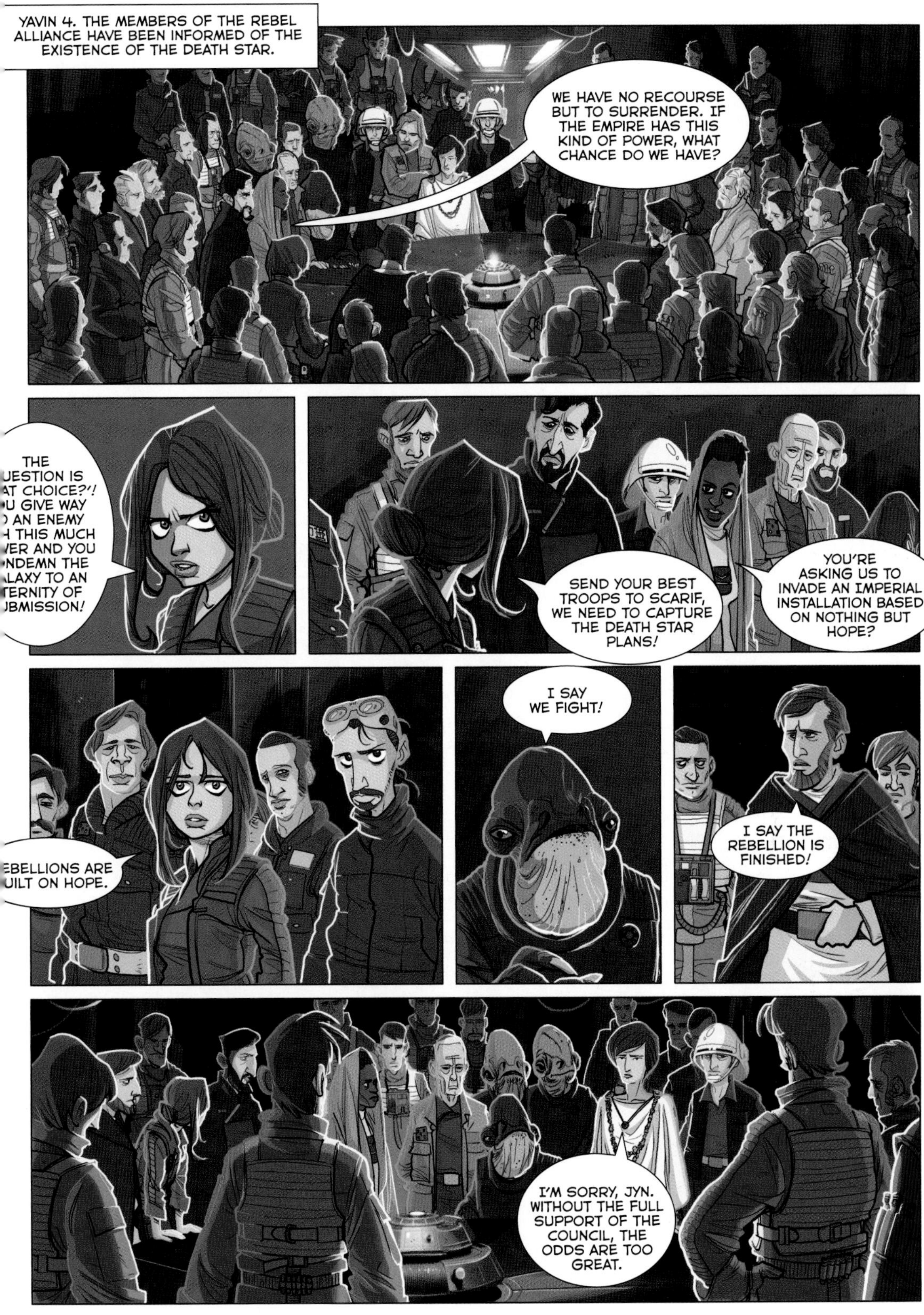
YAVIN 4. THE MEMBERS OF THE REBEL ALLIANCE HAVE BEEN INFORMED OF THE EXISTENCE OF THE DEATH STAR.
WE HAVE NO RECOURSE BUT TO SURRENDER. IF THE EMPIRE HAS THIS KIND OF POWER, WHAT CHANCE DO WE HAVE?
THE UESTION IS AT CHOICE?'! U GIVE WAY AN ENEMY H THIS MUCH ER AND YOU NDEMN THE LAXY TO AN TERNITY OF UBMISSION!
SEND YOUR BEST TROOPS TO SCARIF, WE NEED TO CAPTURE THE DEATH STAR PLANS!
YOU'RE ASKING US TO INVADE AN IMPERIAL INSTALLATION BASED ON NOTHING BUT HOPE?
EBELLIONS ARE UILT ON HOPE.
I SAY WE FIGHT!
I SAY THE REBELLION IS FINISHED!
I'M SORRY, JYN. WITHOUT THE FULL SUPPORT OF THE COUNCIL, THE ODDS ARE TOO GREAT.

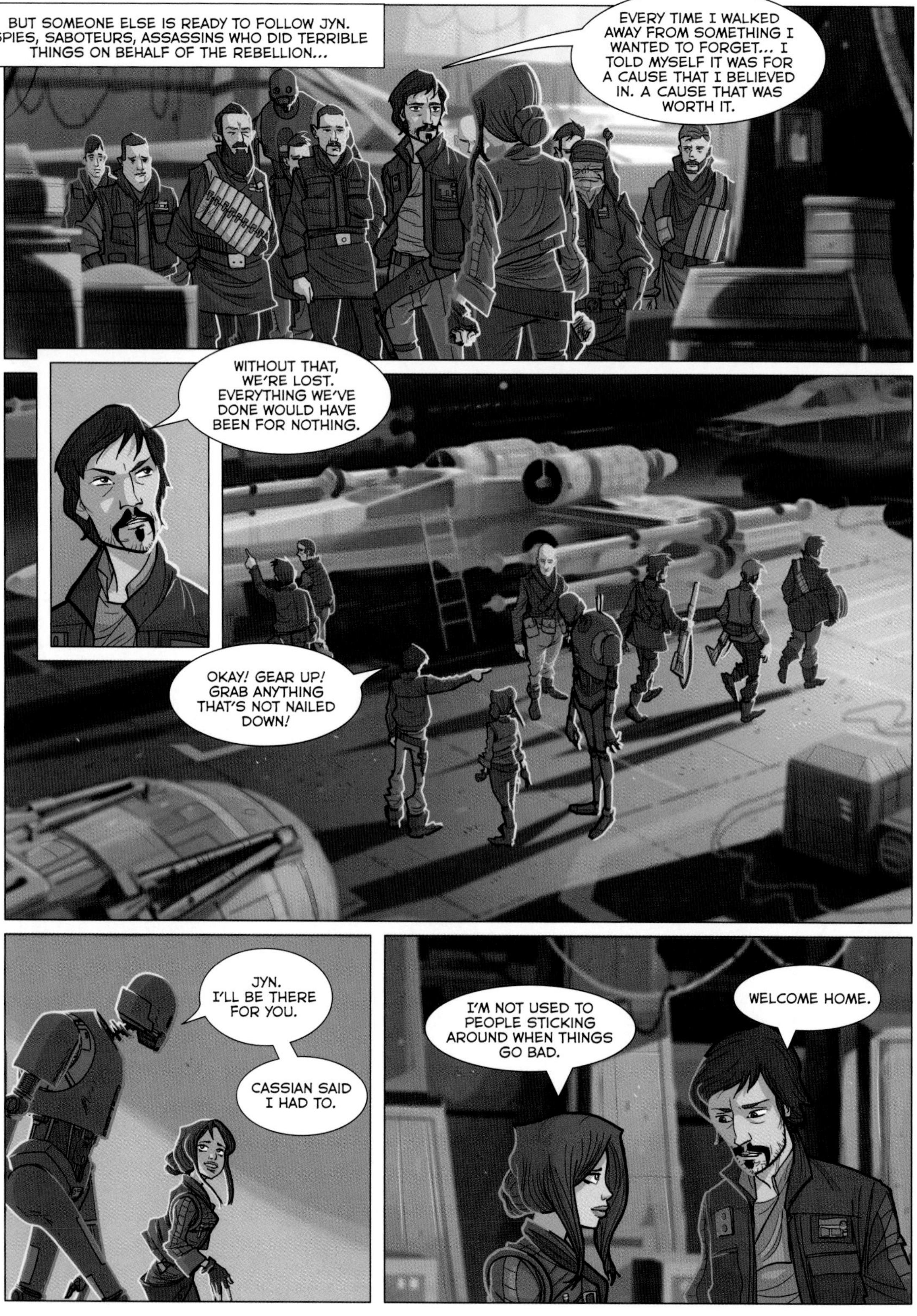
BUT SOMEONE ELSE IS READY TO FOLLOW JYN. SPIES, SABOTEURS, ASSASSINS WHO DID TERRIBLE THINGS ON BEHALF OF THE REBELLION...
EVERY TIME I WALKED AWAY FROM SOMETHING I WANTED TO FORGET... I TOLD MYSELF IT WAS FOR A CAUSE THAT I BELIEVED IN. A CAUSE THAT WAS WORTH IT.
WITHOUT THAT, WE'RE LOST. EVERYTHING WE'VE DONE WOULD HAVE BEEN FOR NOTHING.
OKAY! GEAR UP! GRAB ANYTHING THAT'S NOT NAILED DOWN!
JYN. I'LL BE THERE FOR YOU.
CASSIAN SAID I HAD TO.
I'M NOT USED TO PEOPLE STICKING AROUND WHEN THINGS GO BAD.
WELCOME HOME.

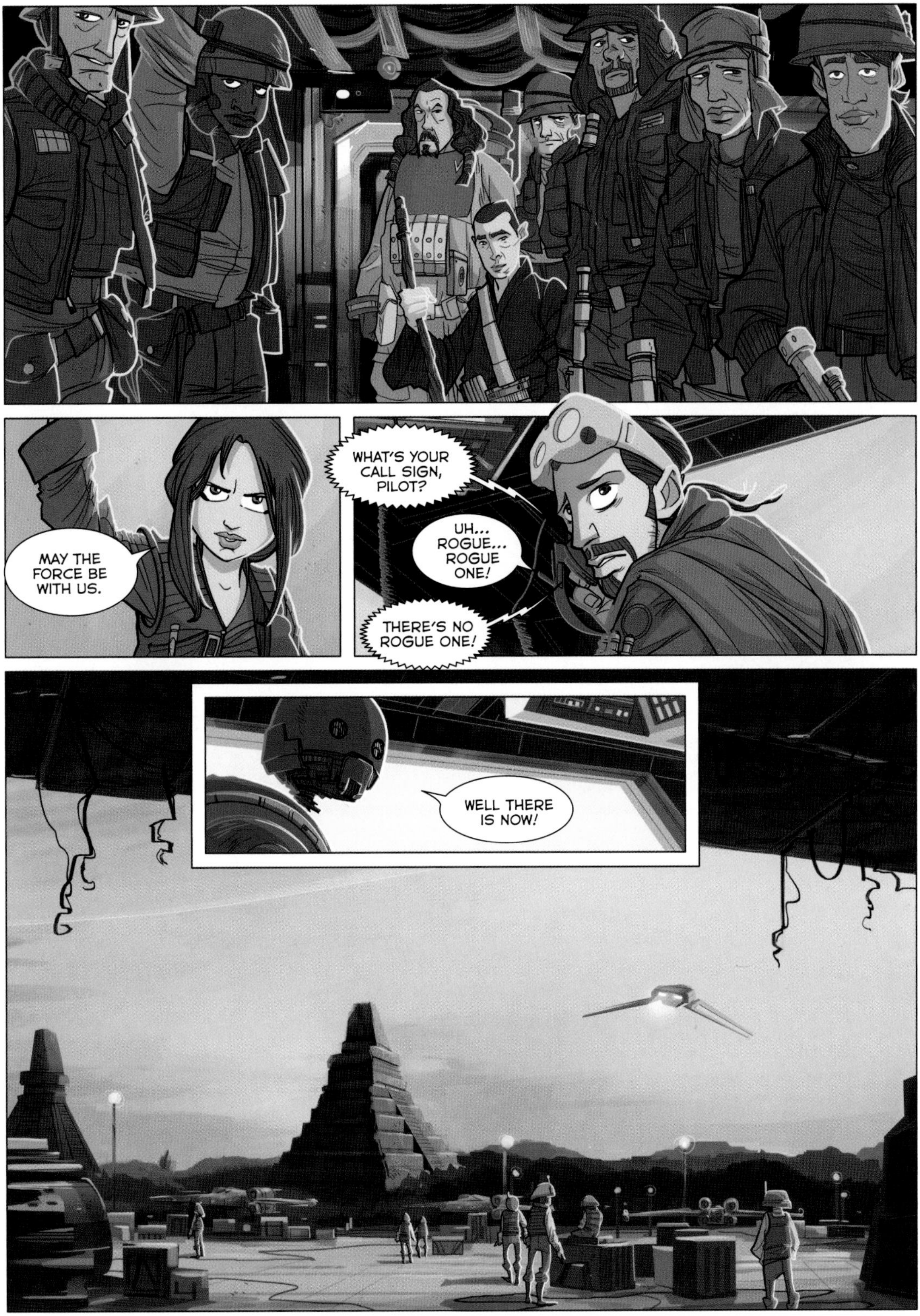

MAY THE FORCE BE WITH US.
WHAT'S YOUR CALL SIGN, PILOT?
UH... ROGUE... ROGUE ONE!
THERE'S NO ROGUE ONE!
WELL THERE IS NOW!

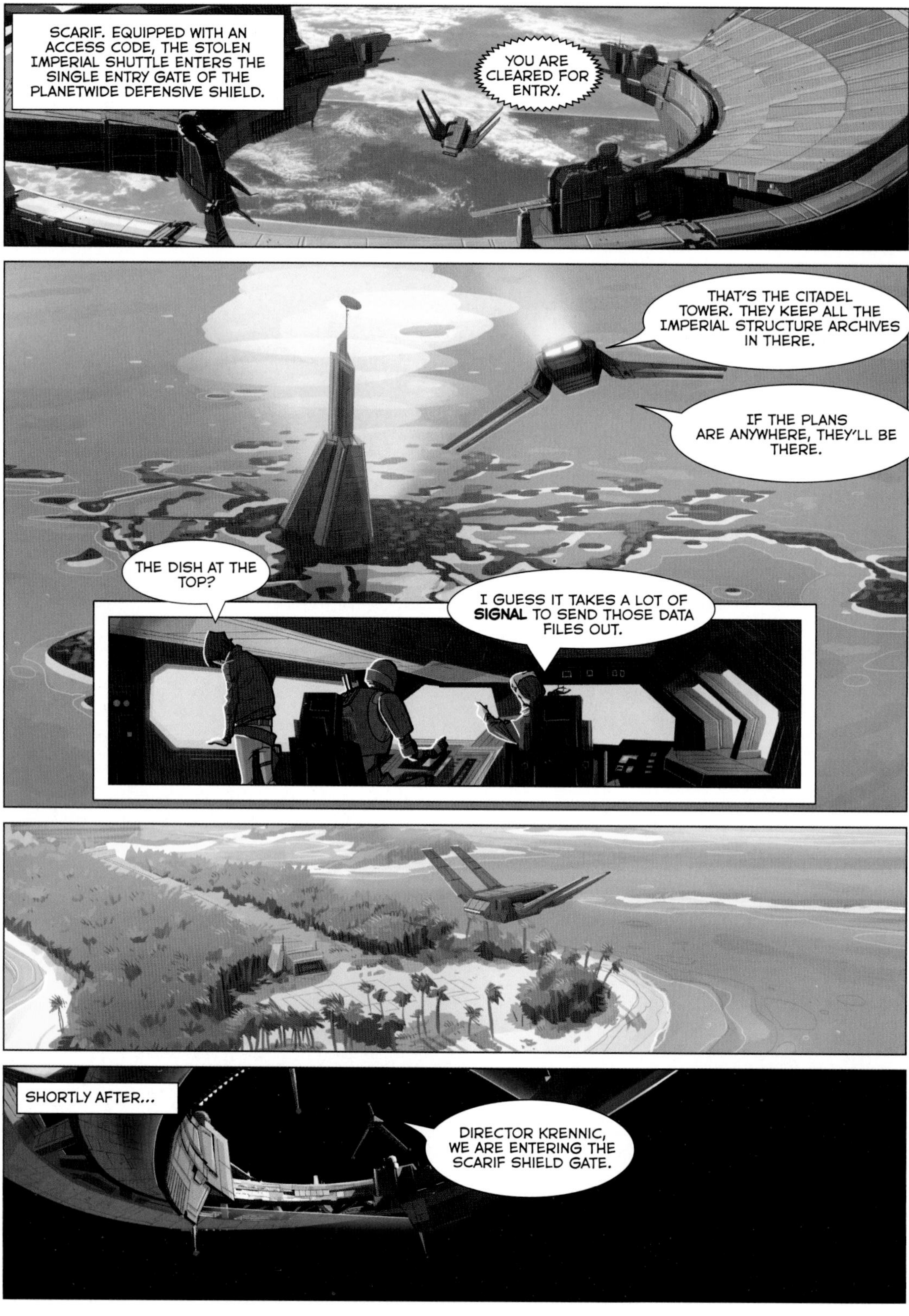
SCARIF. EQUIPPED WITH AN ACCESS CODE, THE STOLEN IMPERIAL SHUTTLE ENTERS THE SINGLE ENTRY GATE OF THE PLANETWIDE DEFENSIVE SHIELD.
YOU ARE CLEARED FOR ENTRY.
THAT'S THE CITADEL TOWER. THEY KEEP ALL THE IMPERIAL STRUCTURE ARCHIVES IN THERE.
IF THE PLANS ARE ANYWHERE, THEY'LL BE THERE.
THE DISH AT THE TOP?
I GUESS IT TAKES A LOT OF **SIGNAL** TO SEND THOSE DATA FILES OUT.
SHORTLY AFTER...
DIRECTOR KRENNIC, WE ARE ENTERING THE SCARIF SHIELD GATE.

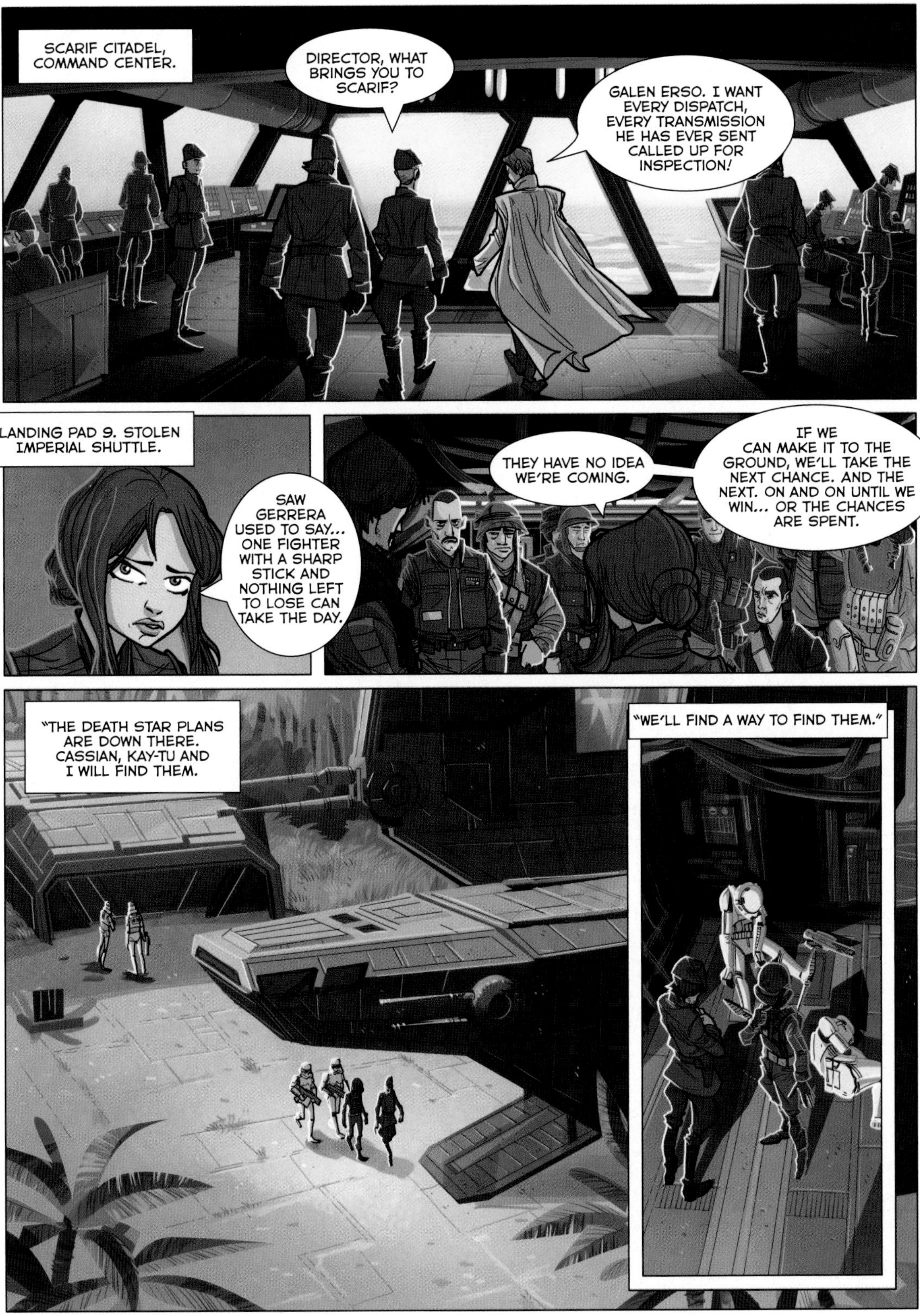
SCARIF CITADEL, COMMAND CENTER.
DIRECTOR, WHAT BRINGS YOU TO SCARIF?
GALEN ERSO. I WANT EVERY DISPATCH, EVERY TRANSMISSION HE HAS EVER SENT CALLED UP FOR INSPECTION!
LANDING PAD 9. STOLEN IMPERIAL SHUTTLE.
SAW GERRERA USED TO SAY... ONE FIGHTER WITH A SHARP STICK AND NOTHING LEFT TO LOSE CAN TAKE THE DAY.
THEY HAVE NO IDEA WE'RE COMING.
IF WE CAN MAKE IT TO THE GROUND, WE'LL TAKE THE NEXT CHANCE. AND THE NEXT. ON AND ON UNTIL WE WIN... OR THE CHANCES ARE SPENT.
"THE DEATH STAR PLANS ARE DOWN THERE. CASSIAN, KAY-TU AND I WILL FIND THEM.
"WE'LL FIND A WAY TO FIND THEM."

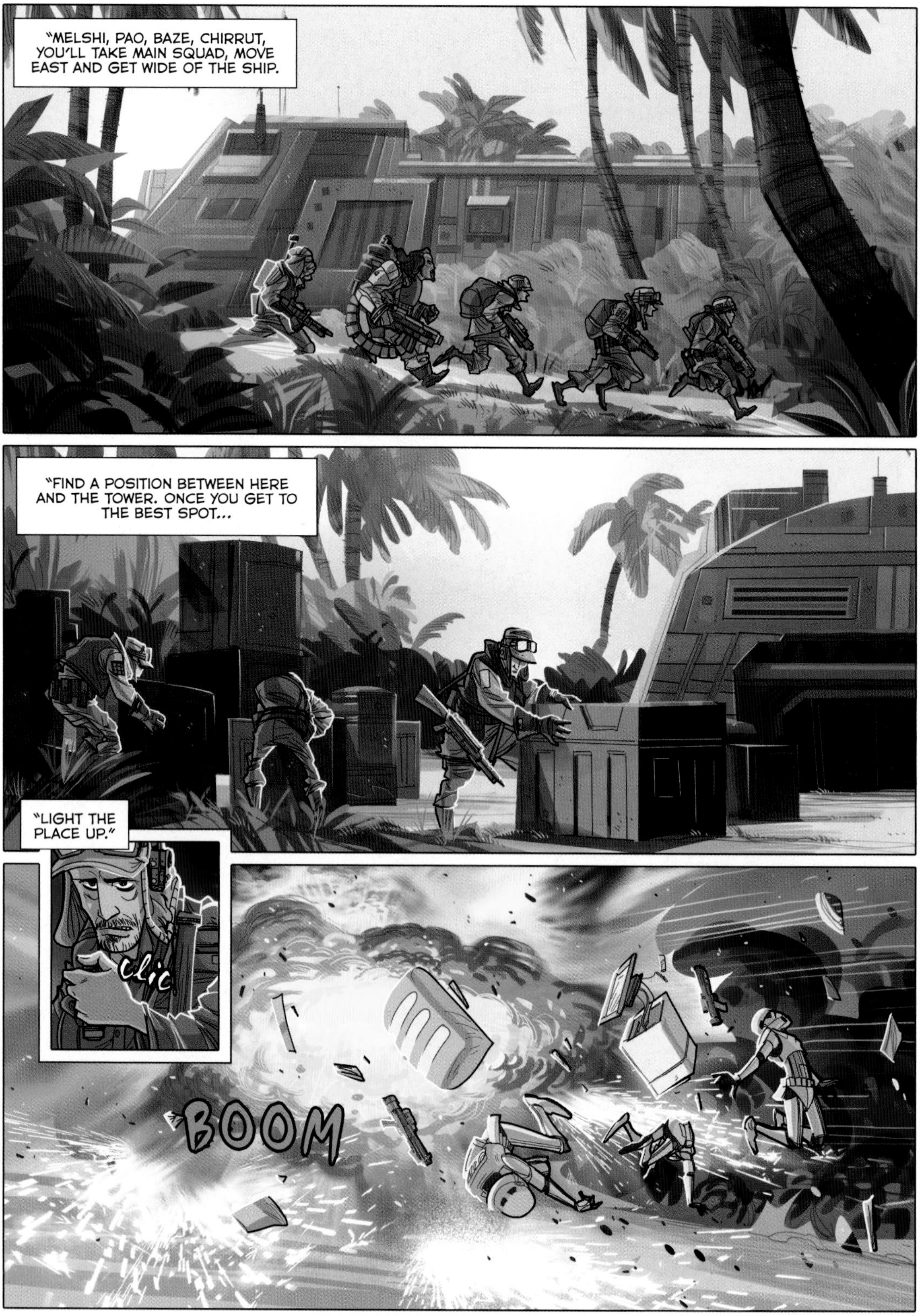
"MELSHI, PAO, BAZE, CHIRRUT, YOU'LL TAKE MAIN SQUAD, MOVE EAST AND GET WIDE OF THE SHIP.
"FIND A POSITION BETWEEN HERE AND THE TOWER. ONCE YOU GET TO THE BEST SPOT...
"LIGHT THE PLACE UP."
clic
BOOM

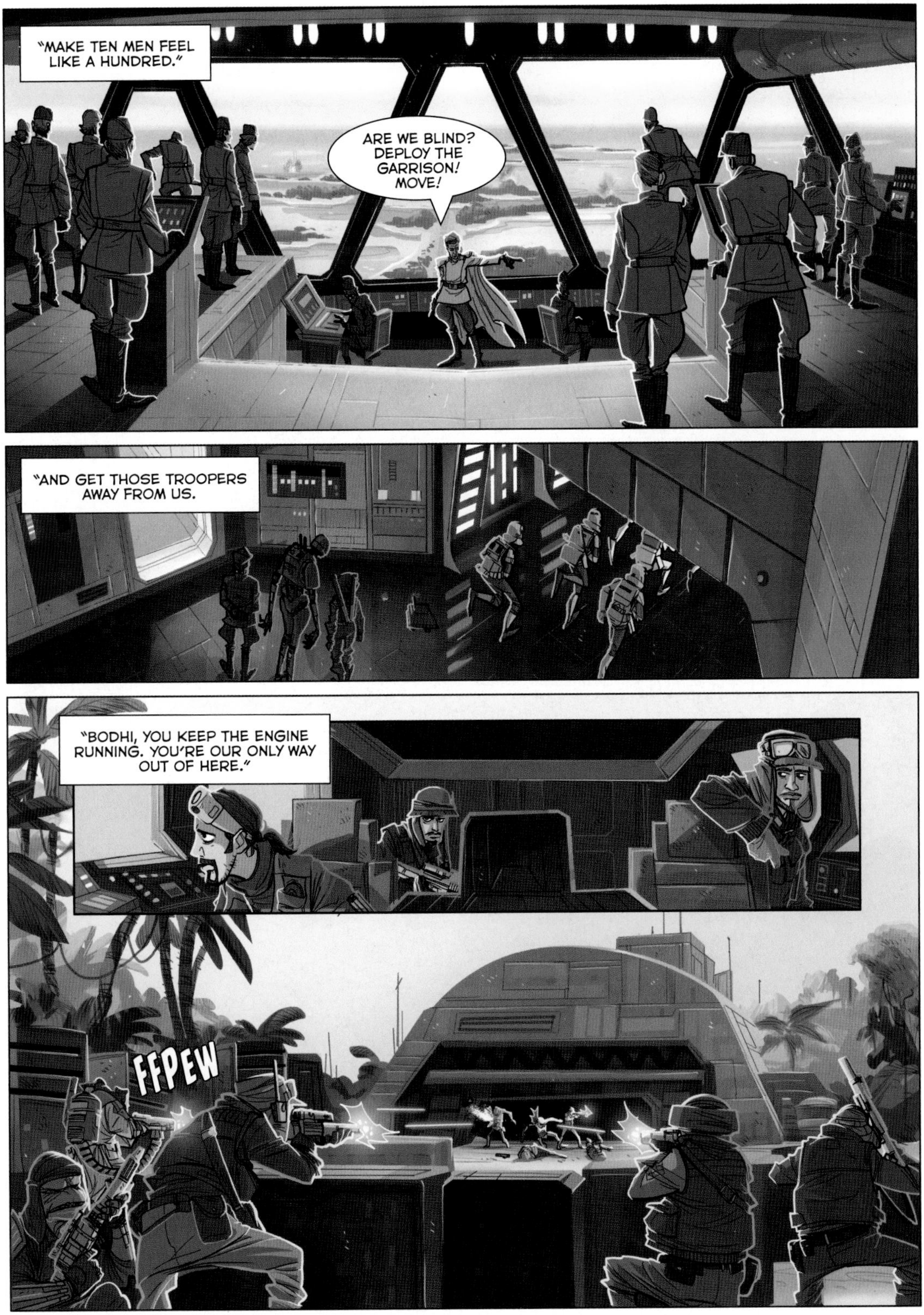
"MAKE TEN MEN FEEL LIKE A HUNDRED."
ARE WE BLIND? DEPLOY THE GARRISON! MOVE!
"AND GET THOSE TROOPERS AWAY FROM US.
"BODHI, YOU KEEP THE ENGINE RUNNING. YOU'RE OUR ONLY WAY OUT OF HERE."
FFPEW

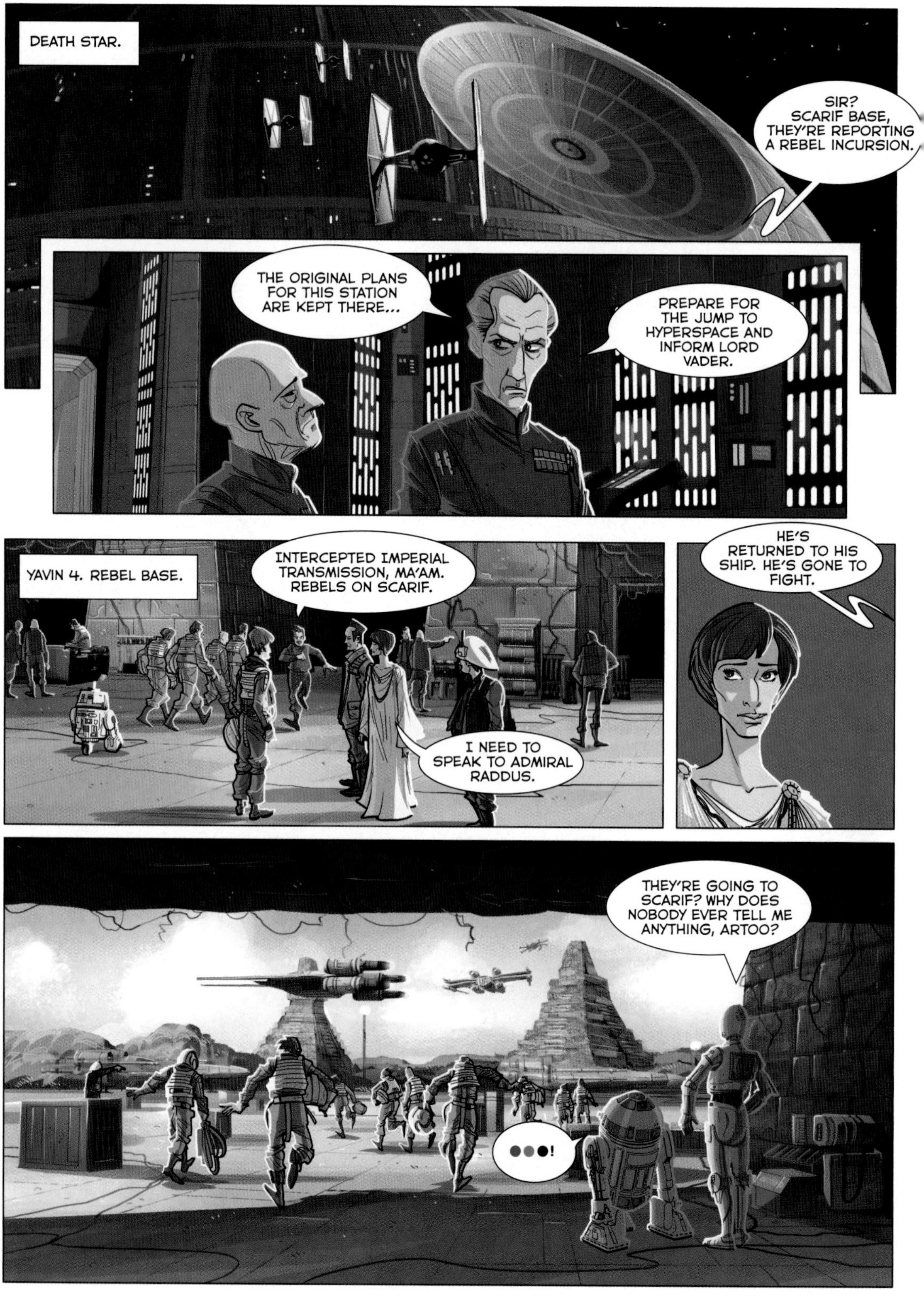
DEATH STAR.
SIR? SCARIF BASE, THEY'RE REPORTING A REBEL INCURSION.
THE ORIGINAL PLANS FOR THIS STATION ARE KEPT THERE...
PREPARE FOR THE JUMP TO HYPERSPACE AND INFORM LORD VADER.
YAVIN 4. REBEL BASE.
INTERCEPTED IMPERIAL TRANSMISSION, MA'AM. REBELS ON SCARIF.
I NEED TO SPEAK TO ADMIRAL RADDUS.
HE'S RETURNED TO HIS SHIP. HE'S GONE TO FIGHT.
THEY'RE GOING TO SCARIF? WHY DOES NOBODY EVER TELL ME ANYTHING, ARTOO?
!

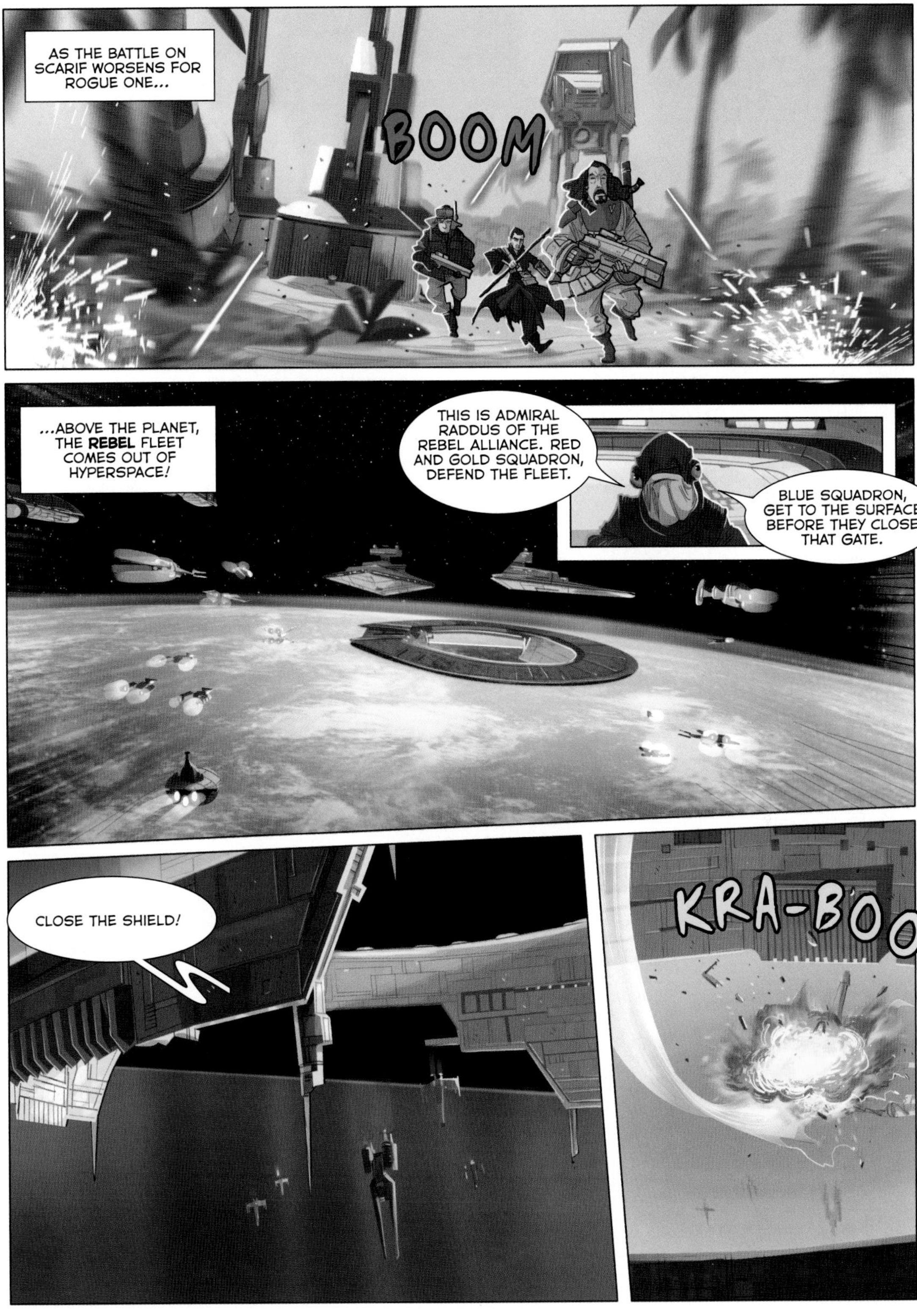
AS THE BATTLE ON SCARIF WORSENS FOR ROGUE ONE...
BOOM
...ABOVE THE PLANET, THE **REBEL** FLEET COMES OUT OF HYPERSPACE!
THIS IS ADMIRAL RADDUS OF THE REBEL ALLIANCE. RED AND GOLD SQUADRON, DEFEND THE FLEET.
BLUE SQUADRON, GET TO THE SURFACE BEFORE THEY CLOSE THAT GATE.
CLOSE THE SHIELD!
KRA-BOOM

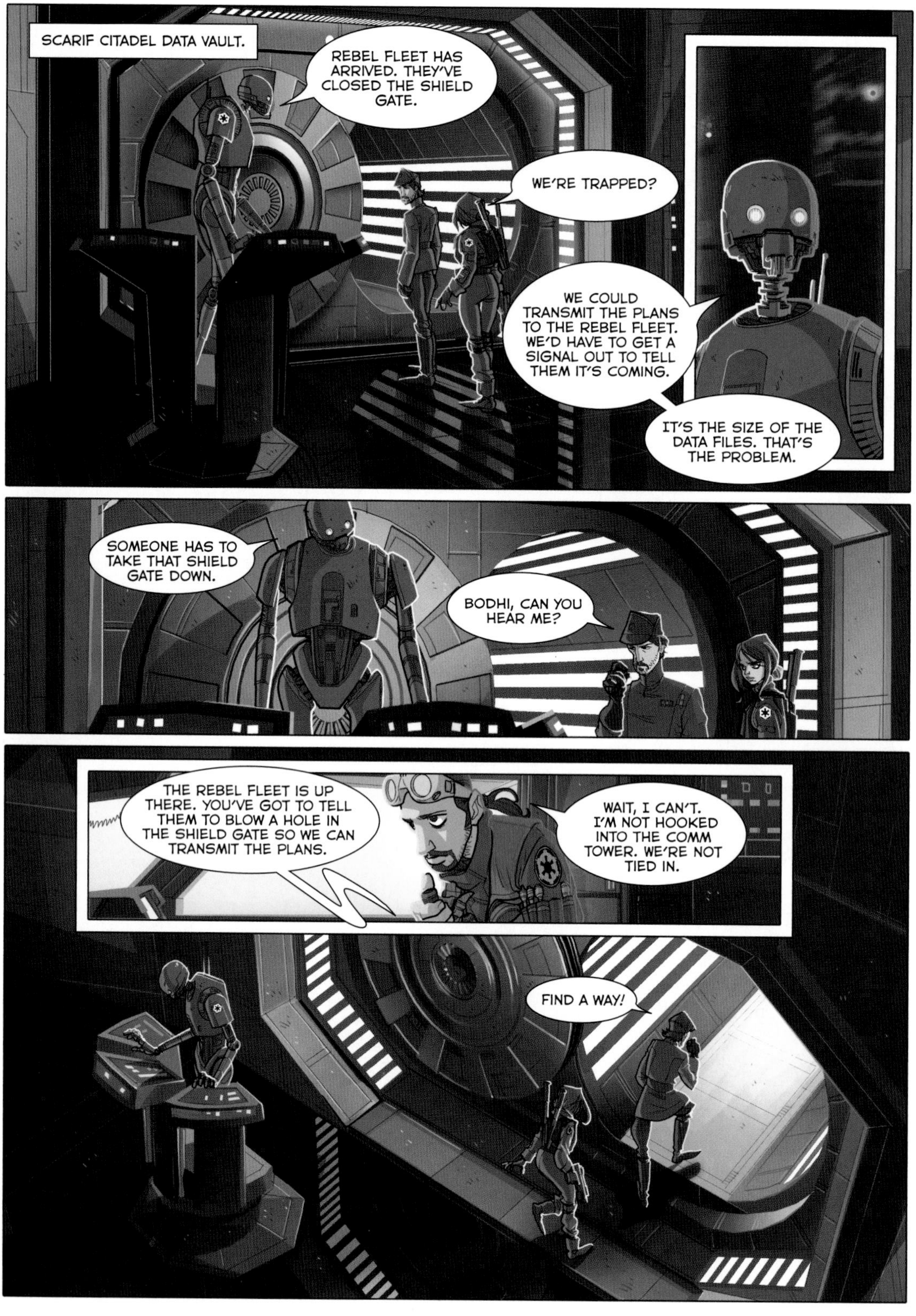
SCARIF CITADEL DATA VAULT.
REBEL FLEET HAS ARRIVED. THEY'VE CLOSED THE SHIELD GATE.
WE'RE TRAPPED?
WE COULD TRANSMIT THE PLANS TO THE REBEL FLEET. WE'D HAVE TO GET A SIGNAL OUT TO TELL THEM IT'S COMING.
IT'S THE SIZE OF THE DATA FILES. THAT'S THE PROBLEM.
SOMEONE HAS TO TAKE THAT SHIELD GATE DOWN.
BODHI, CAN YOU HEAR ME?
THE REBEL FLEET IS UP THERE. YOU'VE GOT TO TELL THEM TO BLOW A HOLE IN THE SHIELD GATE SO WE CAN TRANSMIT THE PLANS.
WAIT, I CAN'T. I'M NOT HOOKED INTO THE COMM TOWER. WE'RE NOT TIED IN.
FIND A WAY!

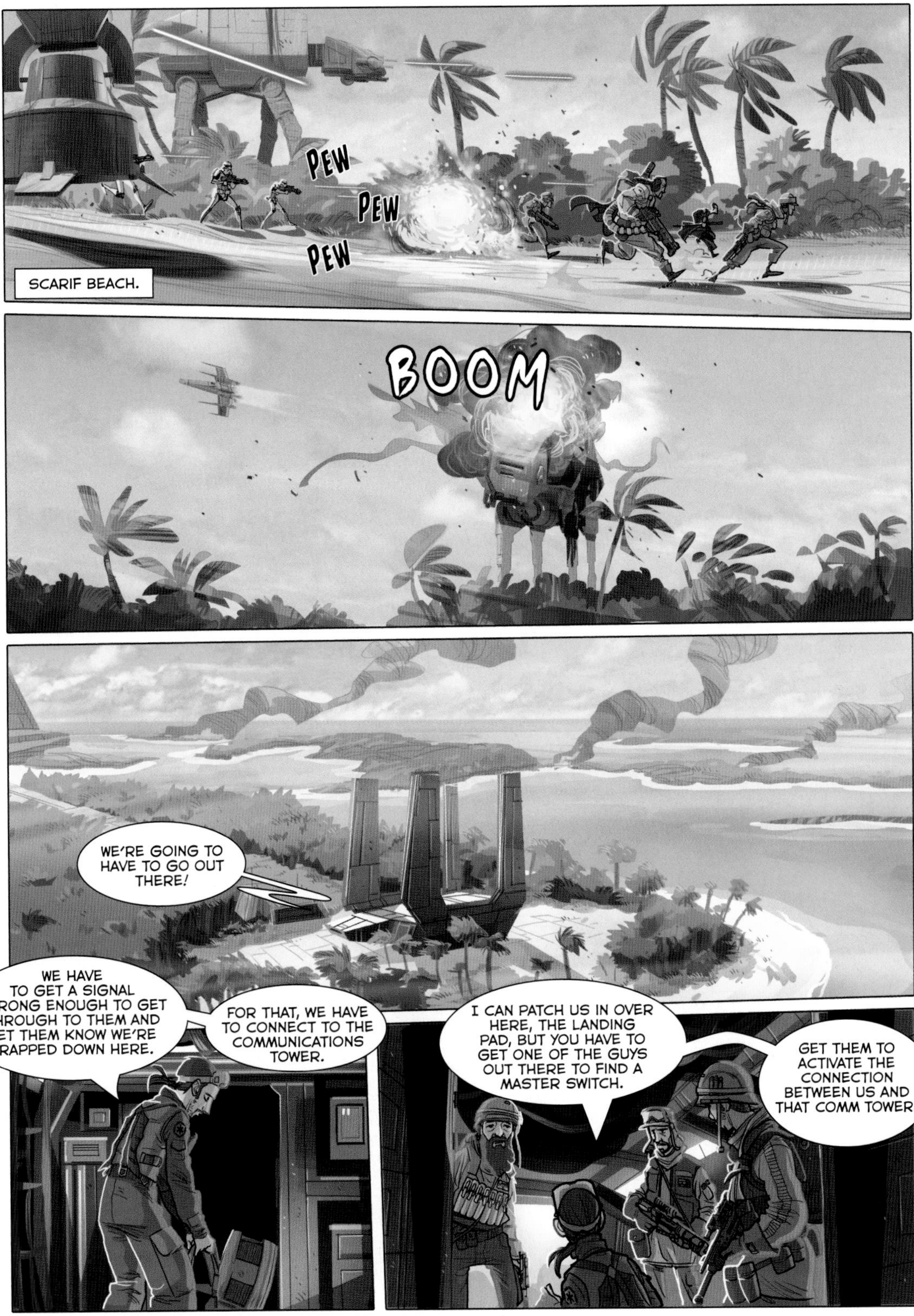
SCARIF BEACH.
PEW
PEW
PEW
BOOM
WE'RE GOING TO HAVE TO GO OUT THERE!
WE HAVE TO GET A SIGNAL STRONG ENOUGH TO GET THROUGH TO THEM AND LET THEM KNOW WE'RE TRAPPED DOWN HERE.
FOR THAT, WE HAVE TO CONNECT TO THE COMMUNICATIONS TOWER.
I CAN PATCH US IN OVER HERE, THE LANDING PAD, BUT YOU HAVE TO GET ONE OF THE GUYS OUT THERE TO FIND A MASTER SWITCH.
GET THEM TO ACTIVATE THE CONNECTION BETWEEN US AND THAT COMM TOWER.

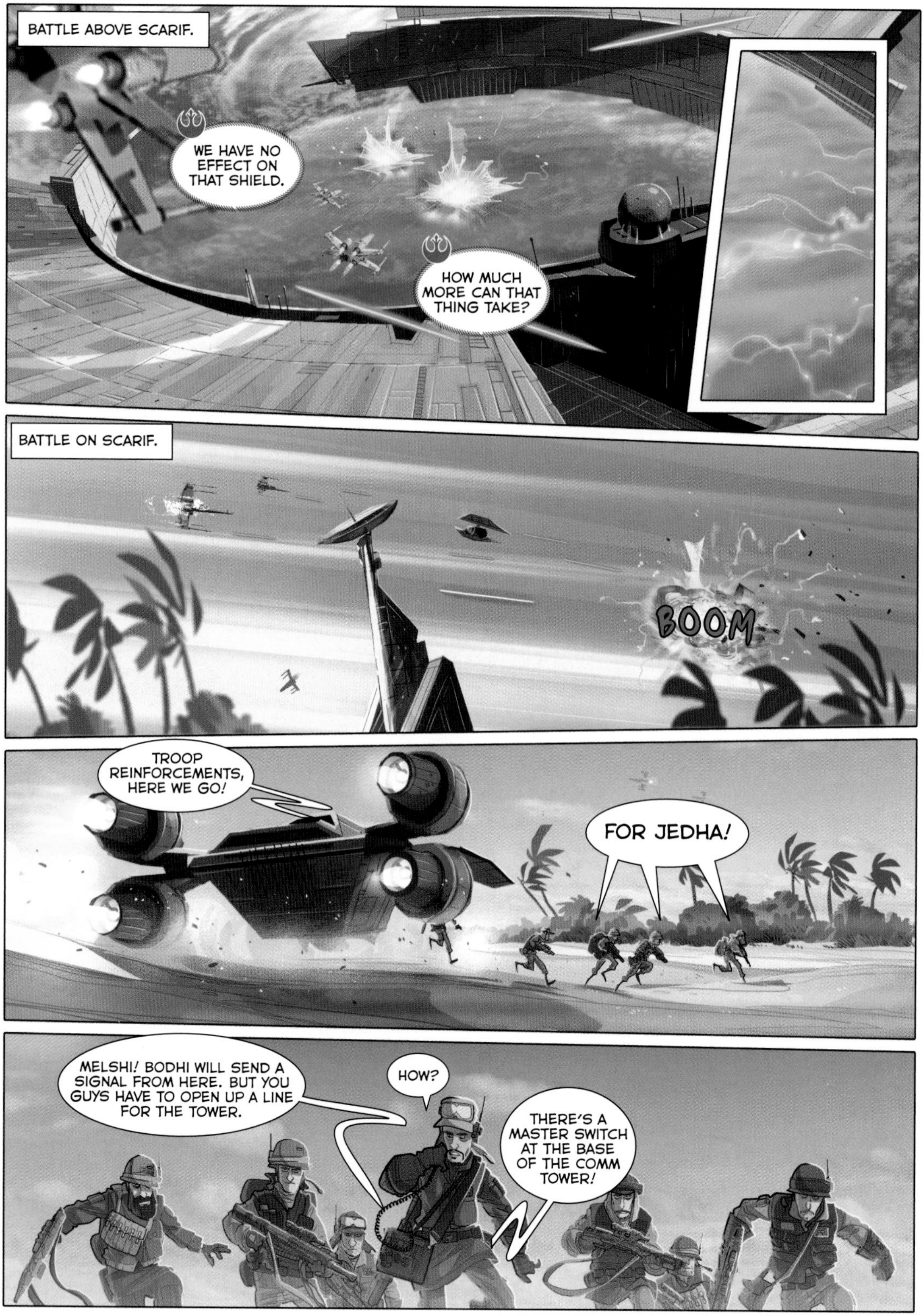
BATTLE ABOVE SCARIF.
WE HAVE NO EFFECT ON THAT SHIELD.
HOW MUCH MORE CAN THAT THING TAKE?
BATTLE ON SCARIF.
BOOM
TROOP REINFORCEMENTS, HERE WE GO!
FOR JEDHA!
MELSHI! BODHI WILL SEND A SIGNAL FROM HERE. BUT YOU GUYS HAVE TO OPEN UP A LINE FOR THE TOWER.
HOW?
THERE'S A MASTER SWITCH AT THE BASE OF THE COMM TOWER!

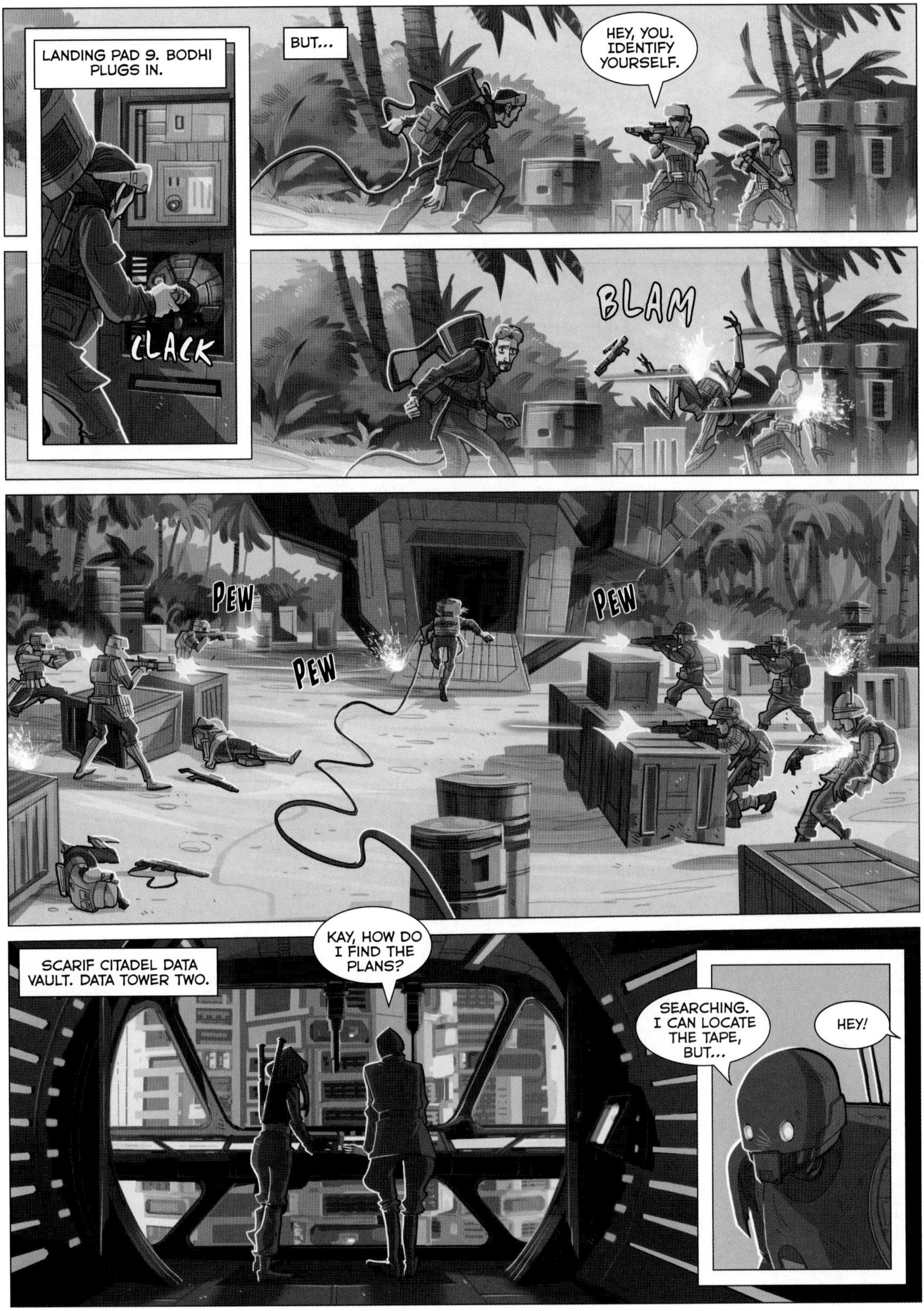
LANDING PAD 9. BODHI PLUGS IN.
CLACK
BUT...
HEY, YOU. IDENTIFY YOURSELF.
BLAM
PEW
PEW
PEW
SCARIF CITADEL DATA VAULT. DATA TOWER TWO.
KAY, HOW DO I FIND THE PLANS?
SEARCHING. I CAN LOCATE THE TAPE, BUT...
HEY!

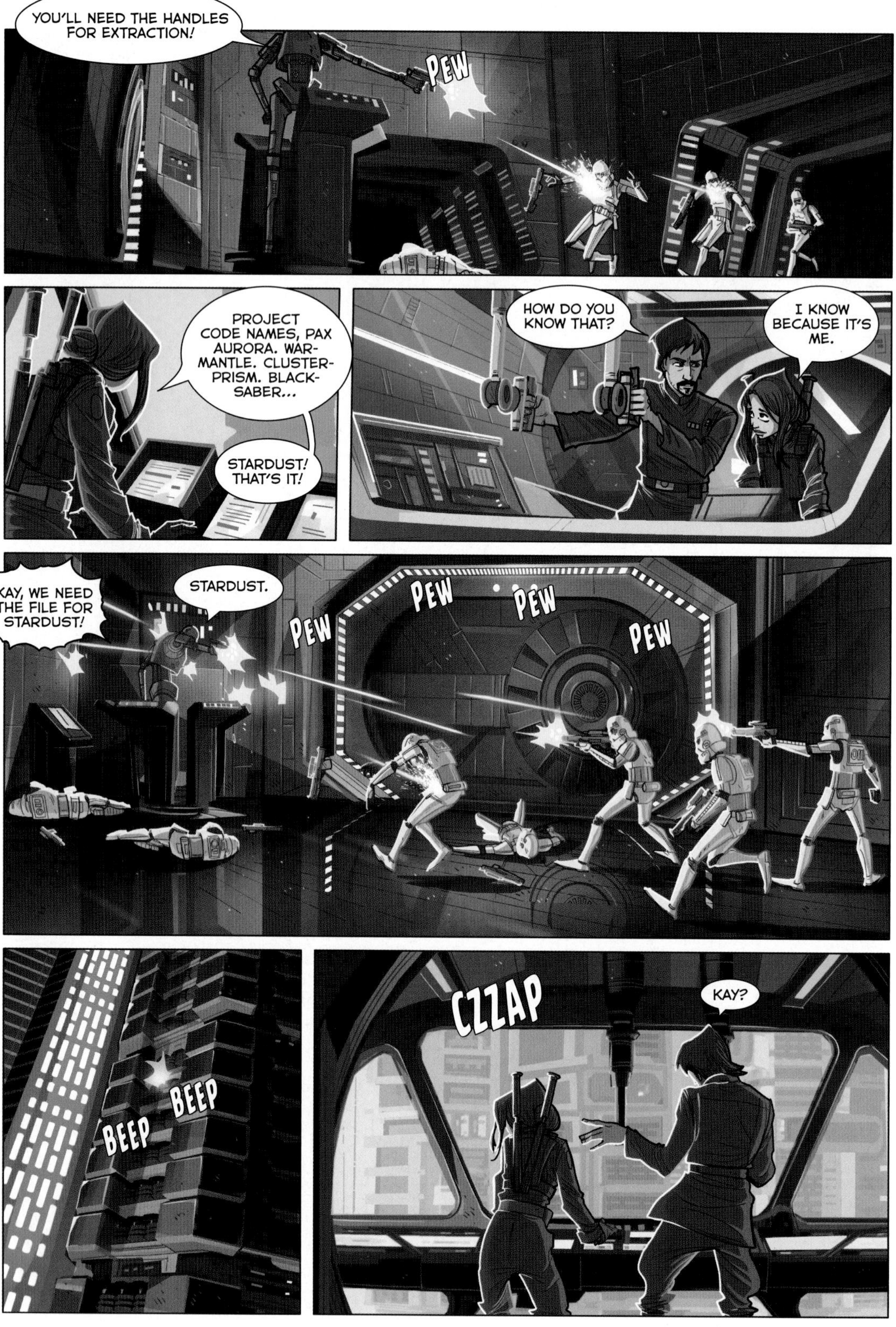
YOU'LL NEED THE HANDLES FOR EXTRACTION!
PEW
PROJECT CODE NAMES, PAX AURORA. WAR-MANTLE. CLUSTER-PRISM. BLACK-SABER...
STARDUST! THAT'S IT!
HOW DO YOU KNOW THAT?
I KNOW BECAUSE IT'S ME.
KAY, WE NEED THE FILE FOR STARDUST!
STARDUST.
PEW
PEW
PEW
PEW
BEEP
BEEP
CZZAP
KAY?

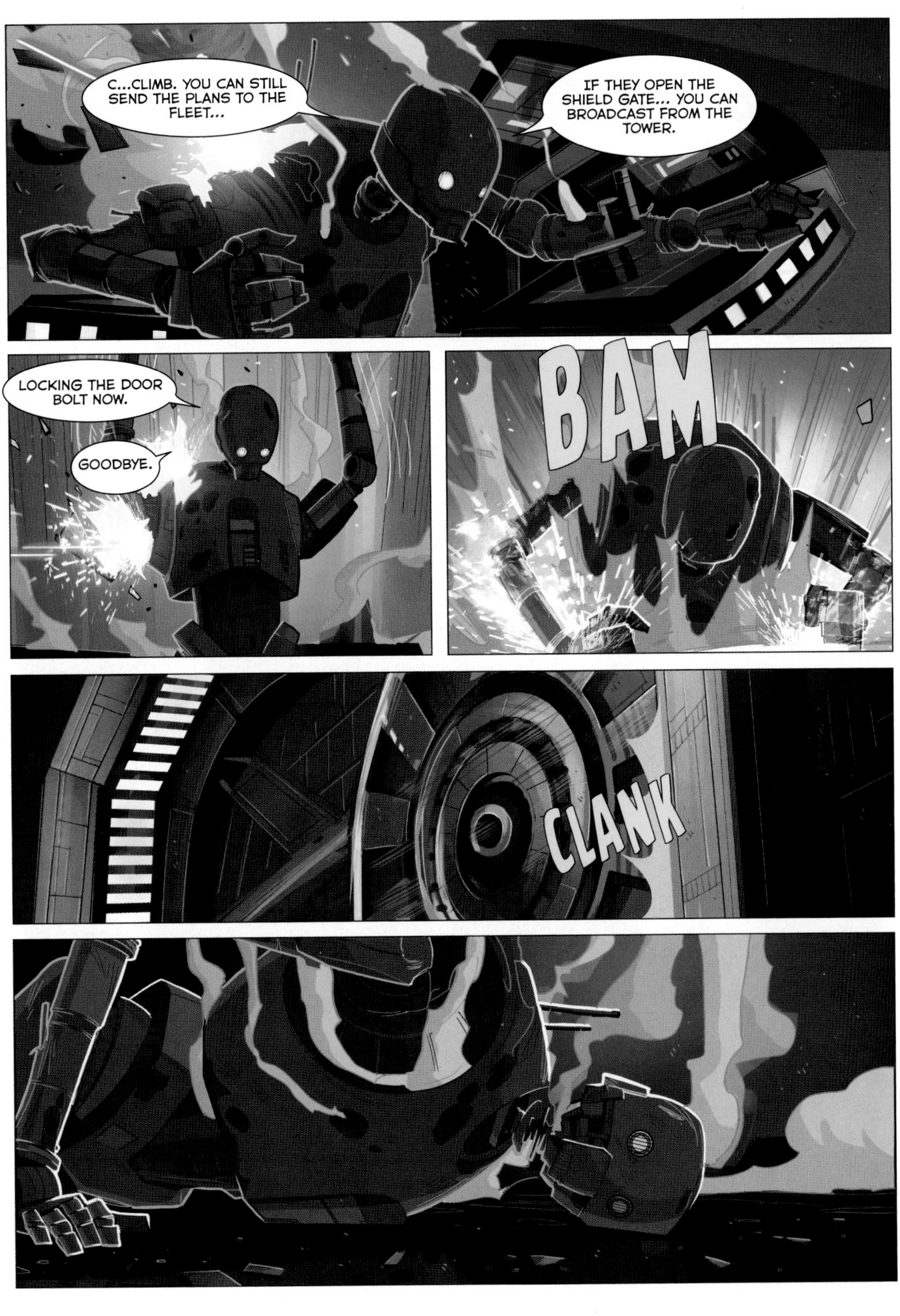
C...CLIMB. YOU CAN STILL SEND THE PLANS TO THE FLEET...
IF THEY OPEN THE SHIELD GATE... YOU CAN BROADCAST FROM THE TOWER.
LOCKING THE DOOR BOLT NOW.
GOODBYE.
BAM
CLANK

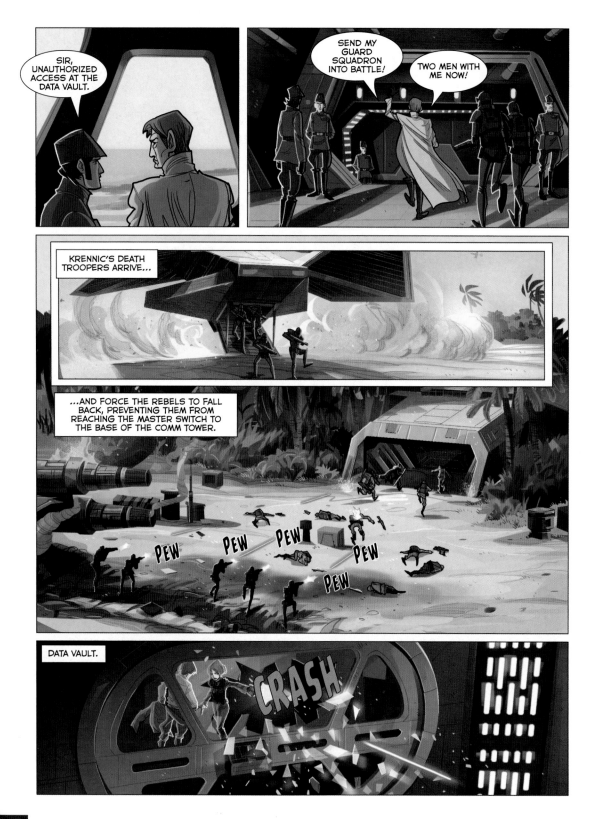

SIR, UNAUTHORIZED ACCESS AT THE DATA VAULT.

SEND MY GUARD SQUADRON INTO BATTLE!

TWO MEN WITH ME NOW!

KRENNIC'S DEATH TROOPERS ARRIVE...

...AND FORCE THE REBELS TO FALL BACK, PREVENTING THEM FROM REACHING THE MASTER SWITCH TO THE BASE OF THE COMM TOWER.

PEW PEW PEW PEW PEW

DATA VAULT.

CRASH

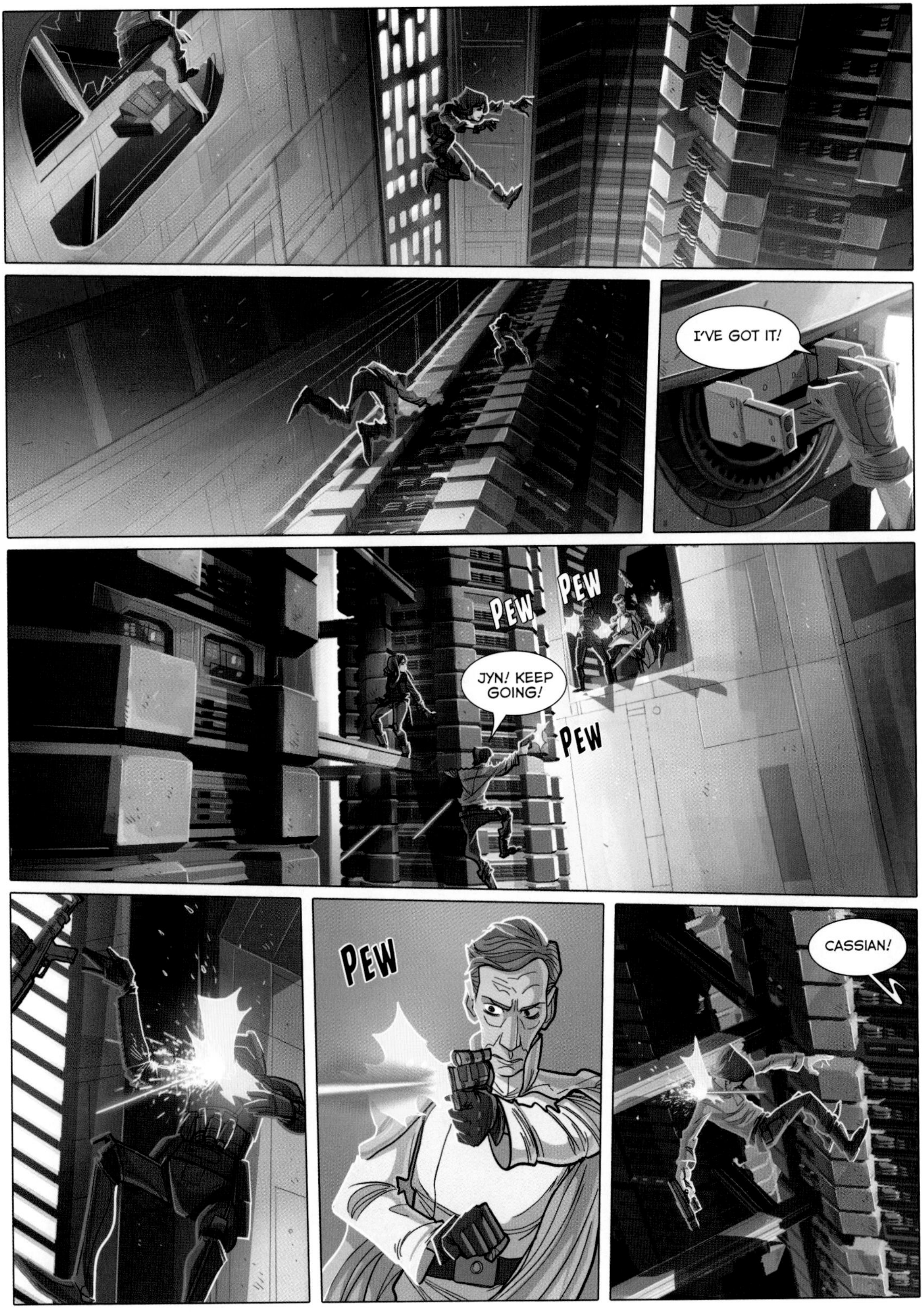
I'VE GOT IT!
PEW
PEW
JYN! KEEP GOING!
PEW
PEW
CASSIAN!

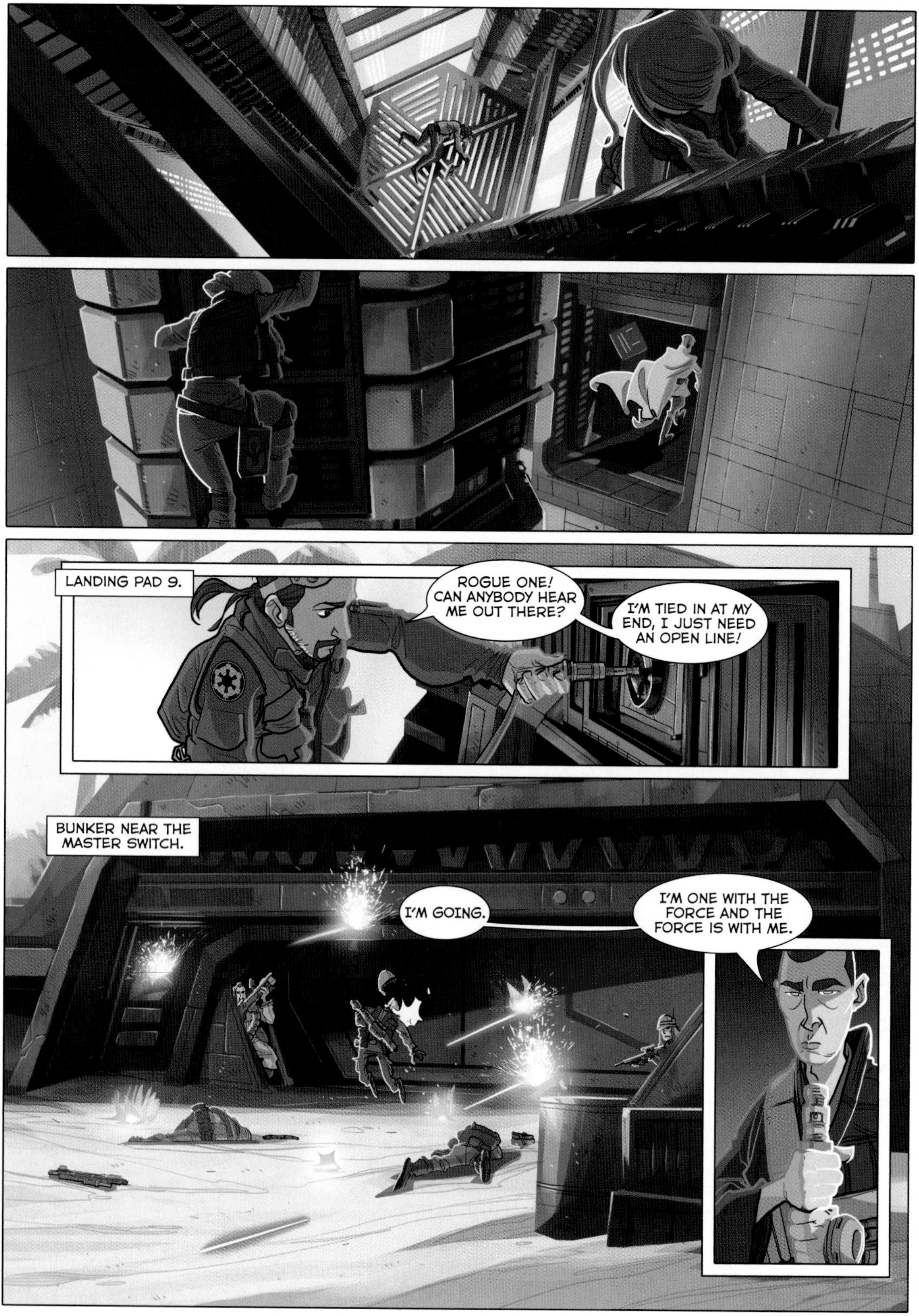

LANDING PAD 9.
ROGUE ONE! CAN ANYBODY HEAR ME OUT THERE?
I'M TIED IN AT MY END, I JUST NEED AN OPEN LINE!
BUNKER NEAR THE MASTER SWITCH.
I'M GOING.
I'M ONE WITH THE FORCE AND THE FORCE IS WITH ME.

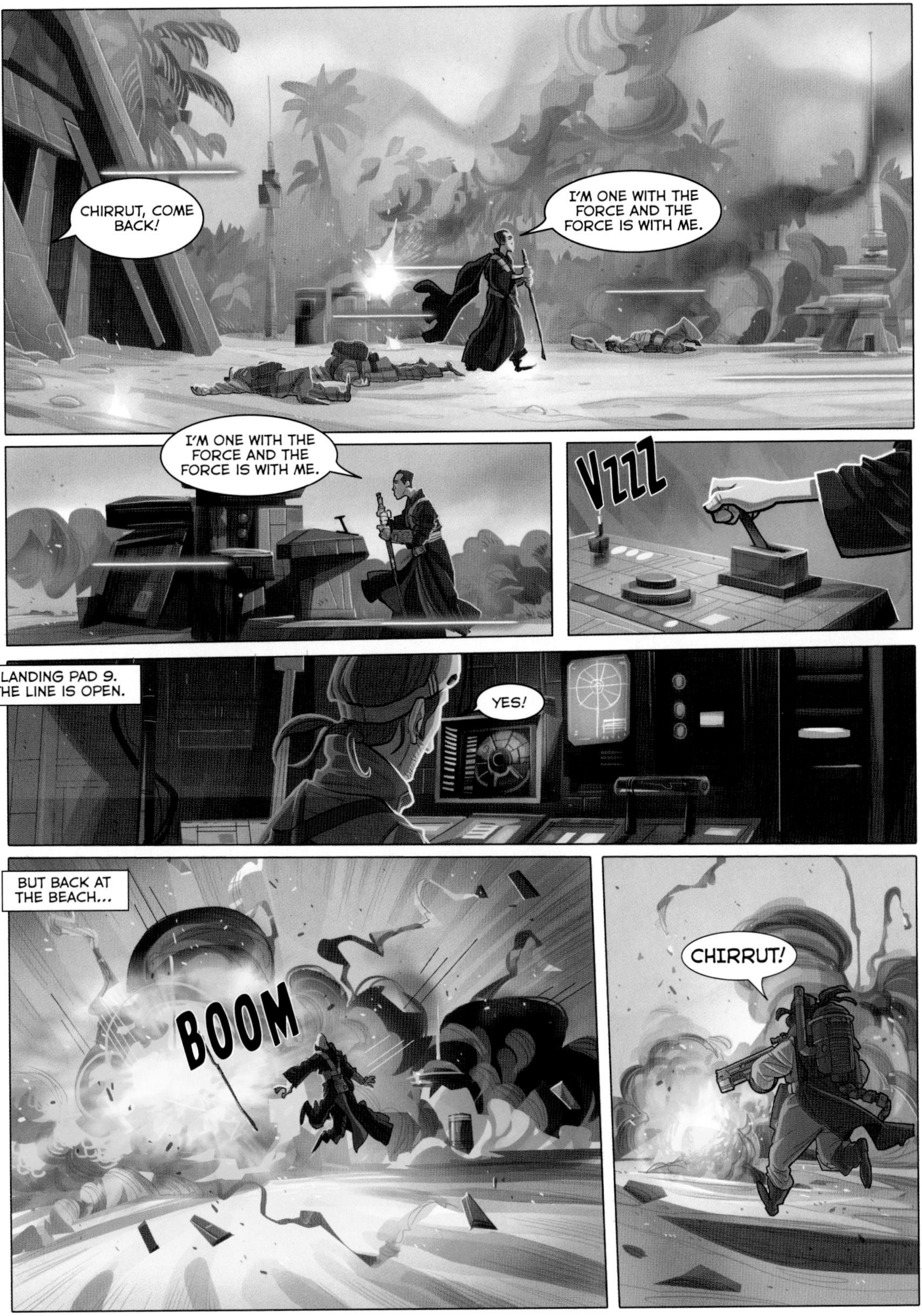
CHIRRUT, COME BACK!
I'M ONE WITH THE FORCE AND THE FORCE IS WITH ME.
I'M ONE WITH THE FORCE AND THE FORCE IS WITH ME.
VZZZ
LANDING PAD 9. THE LINE IS OPEN.
YES!
BUT BACK AT THE BEACH...
BOOM
CHIRRUT!

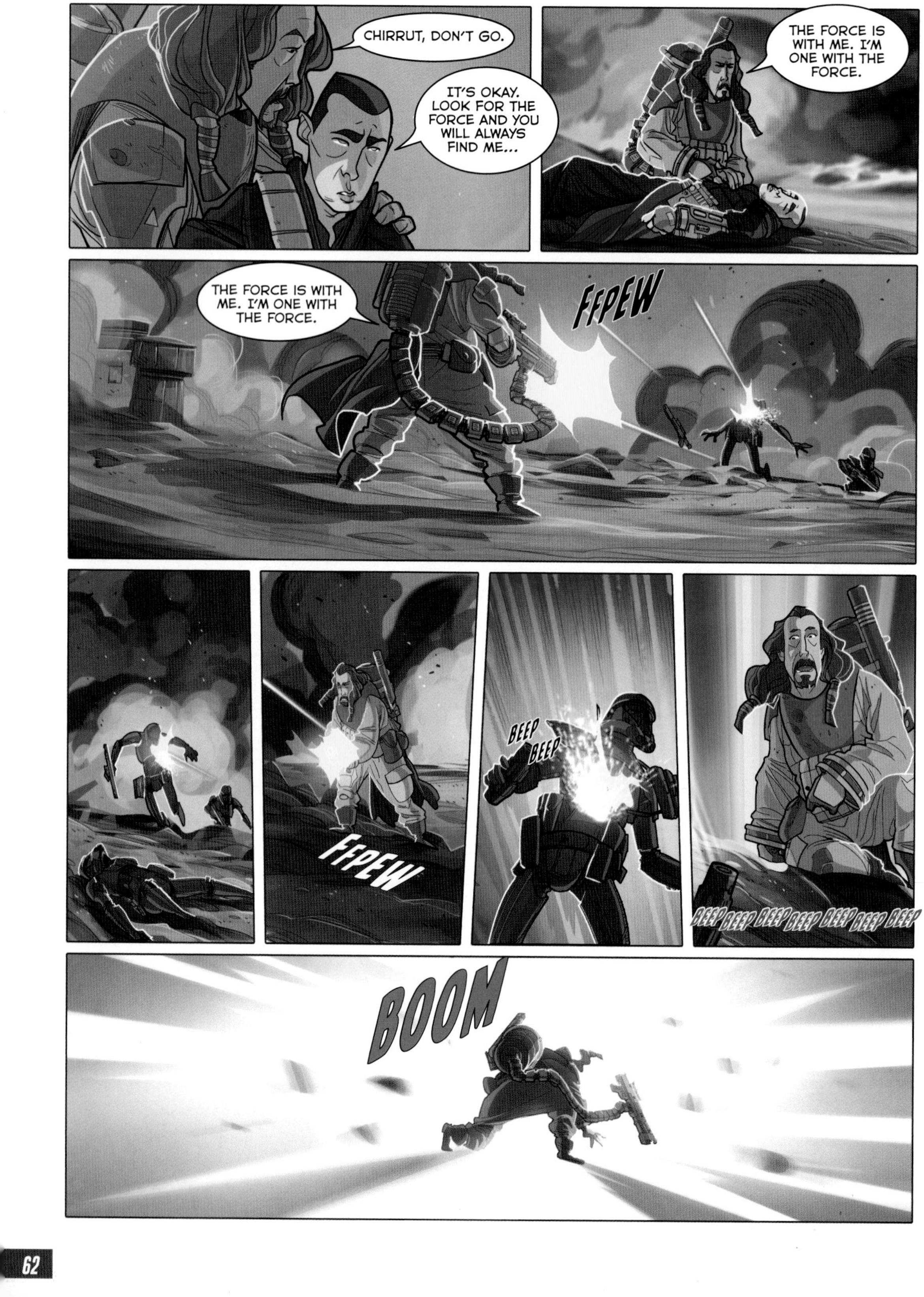
CHIRRUT, DON'T GO.
IT'S OKAY. LOOK FOR THE FORCE AND YOU WILL ALWAYS FIND ME...
THE FORCE IS WITH ME. I'M ONE WITH THE FORCE.
THE FORCE IS WITH ME. I'M ONE WITH THE FORCE.
FFPEW
FFPEW
BEEP BEEP
BEEP BEEP BEEP BEEP BEEP BEEP BEEP
BOOM

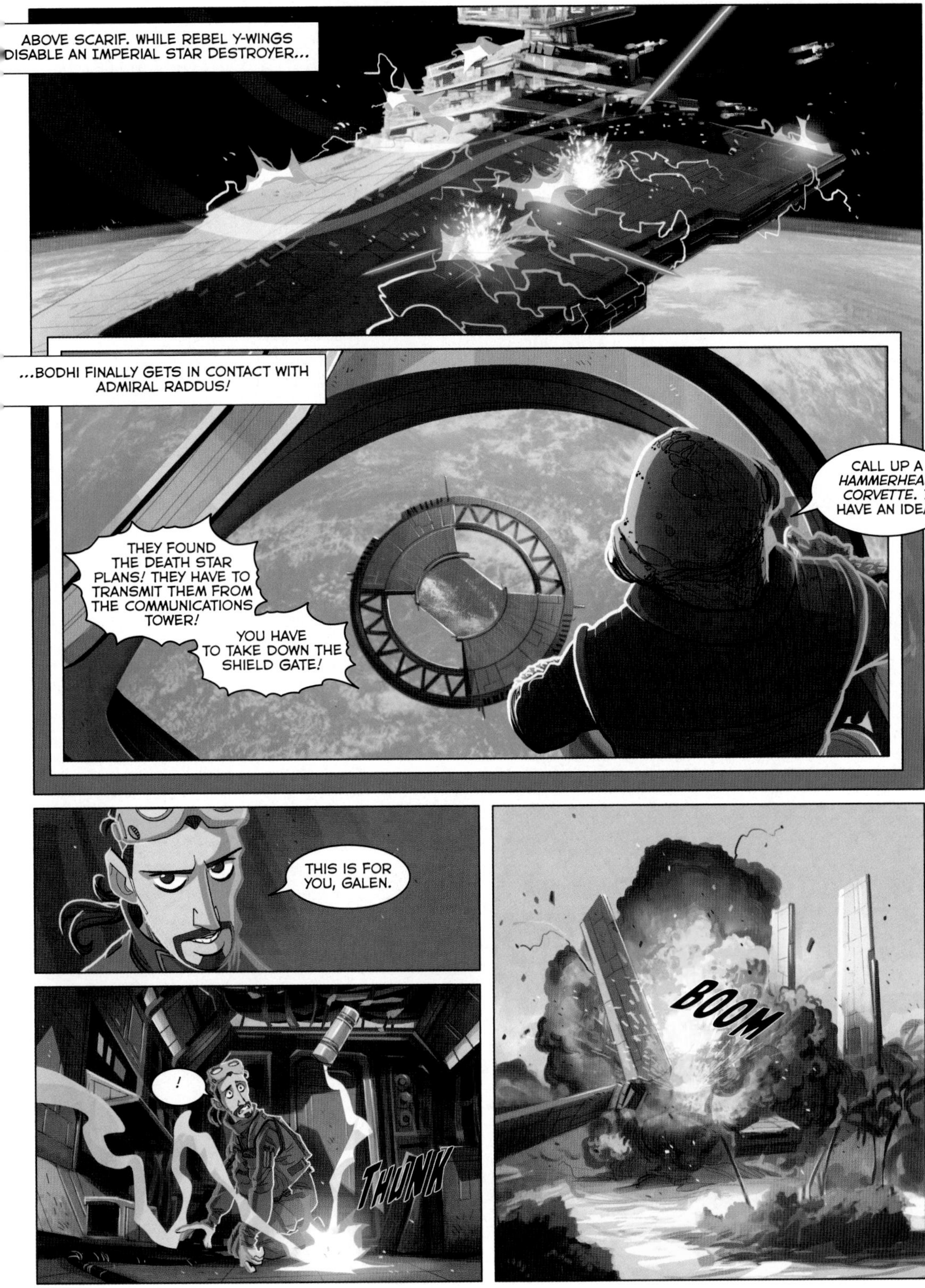

ABOVE SCARIF. WHILE REBEL Y-WINGS DISABLE AN IMPERIAL STAR DESTROYER...
...BODHI FINALLY GETS IN CONTACT WITH ADMIRAL RADDUS!
THEY FOUND THE DEATH STAR PLANS! THEY HAVE TO TRANSMIT THEM FROM THE COMMUNICATIONS TOWER!
YOU HAVE TO TAKE DOWN THE SHIELD GATE!
CALL UP A *HAMMERHEAD CORVETTE*. I HAVE AN IDEA.
THIS IS FOR YOU, GALEN.
!
THUNK
BOOM

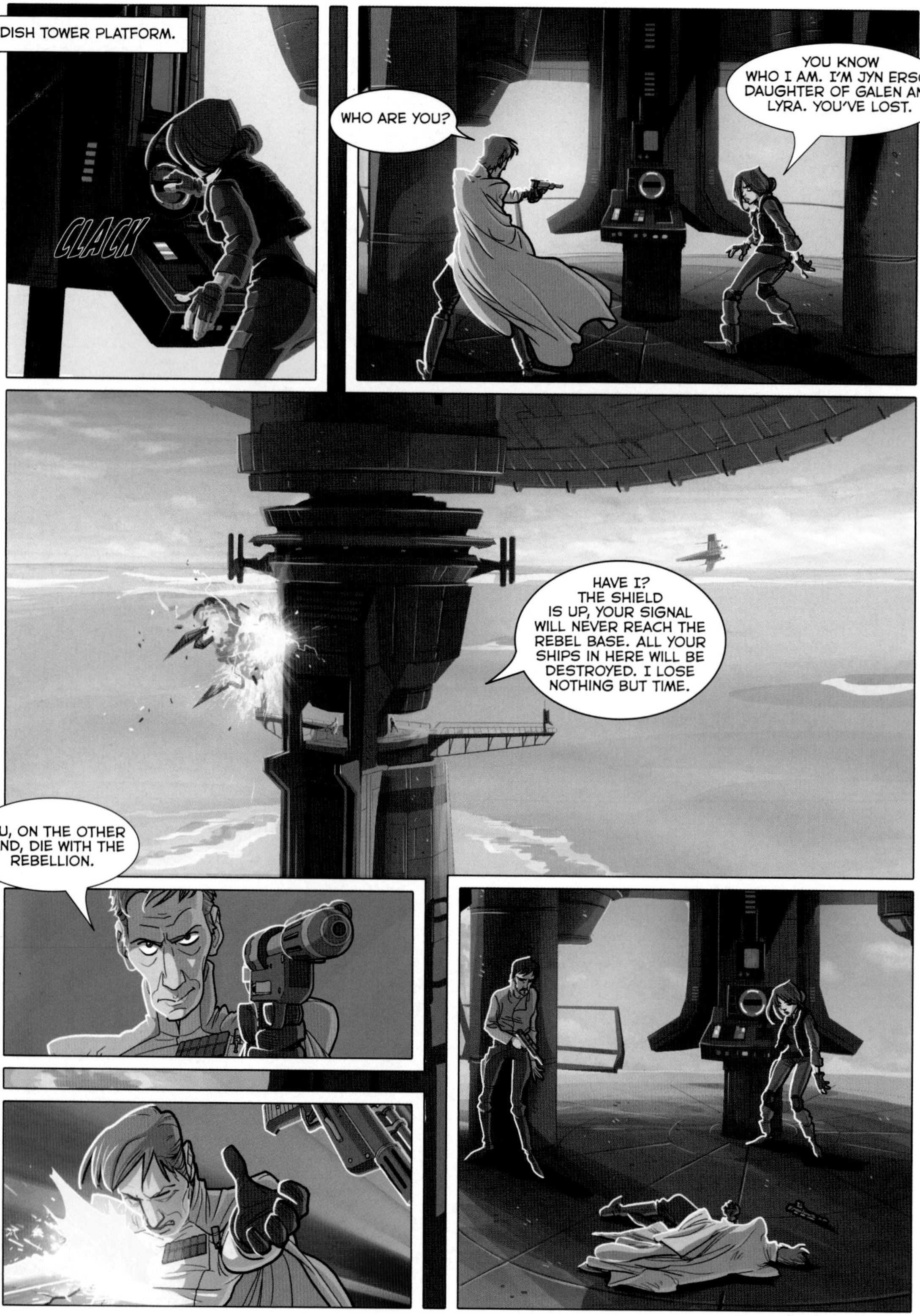
DISH TOWER PLATFORM.
CLACK
WHO ARE YOU?
YOU KNOW WHO I AM. I'M JYN ERSO. DAUGHTER OF GALEN AND LYRA. YOU'VE LOST.
HAVE I? THE SHIELD IS UP, YOUR SIGNAL WILL NEVER REACH THE REBEL BASE. ALL YOUR SHIPS IN HERE WILL BE DESTROYED. I LOSE NOTHING BUT TIME.
YOU, ON THE OTHER HAND, DIE WITH THE REBELLION.

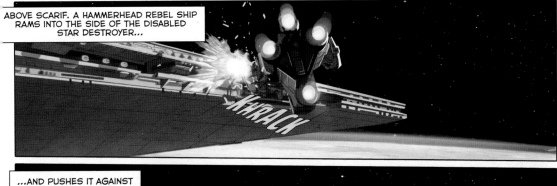

ABOVE SCARIF. A HAMMERHEAD REBEL SHIP RAMS INTO THE SIDE OF THE DISABLED STAR DESTROYER...

KHRACK

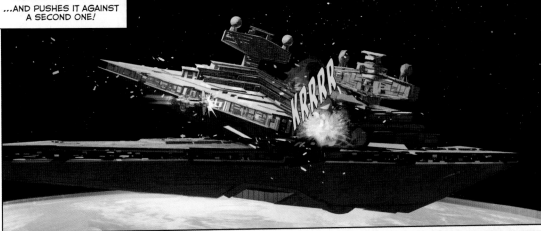

...AND PUSHES IT AGAINST A SECOND ONE!

KRRRR

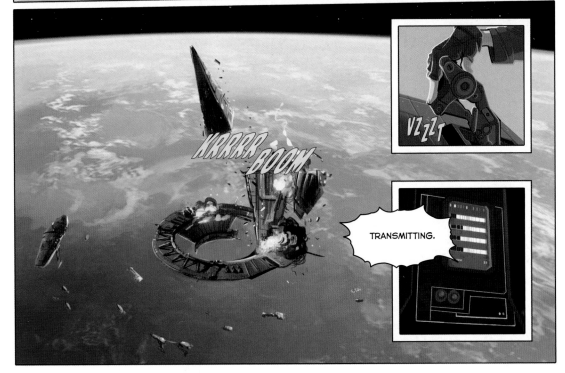

KRRRRR BOOM

VZZZT

TRANSMITTING.

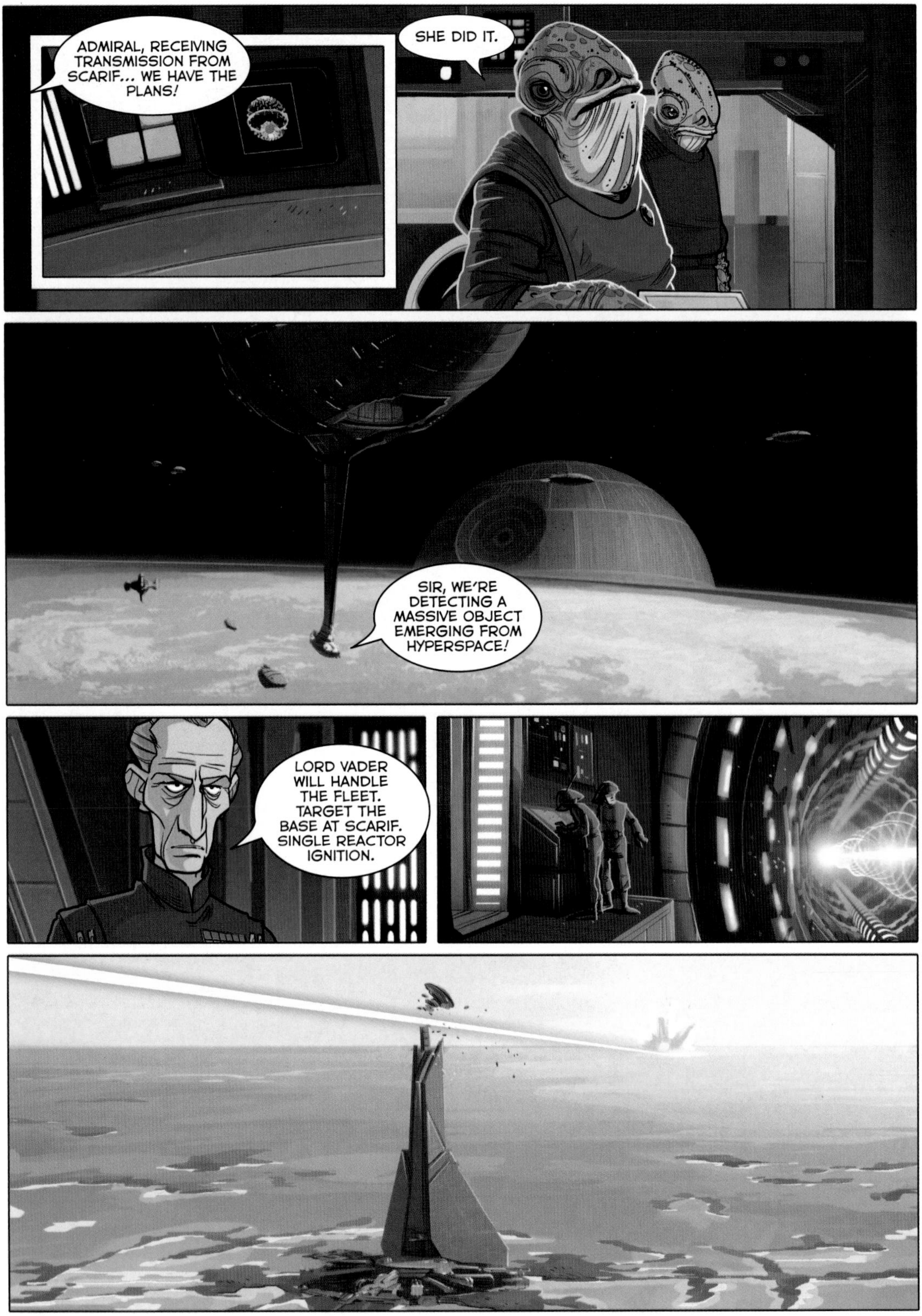
ADMIRAL, RECEIVING TRANSMISSION FROM SCARIF... WE HAVE THE PLANS!
SHE DID IT.
SIR, WE'RE DETECTING A MASSIVE OBJECT EMERGING FROM HYPERSPACE!
LORD VADER WILL HANDLE THE FLEET. TARGET THE BASE AT SCARIF. SINGLE REACTOR IGNITION.

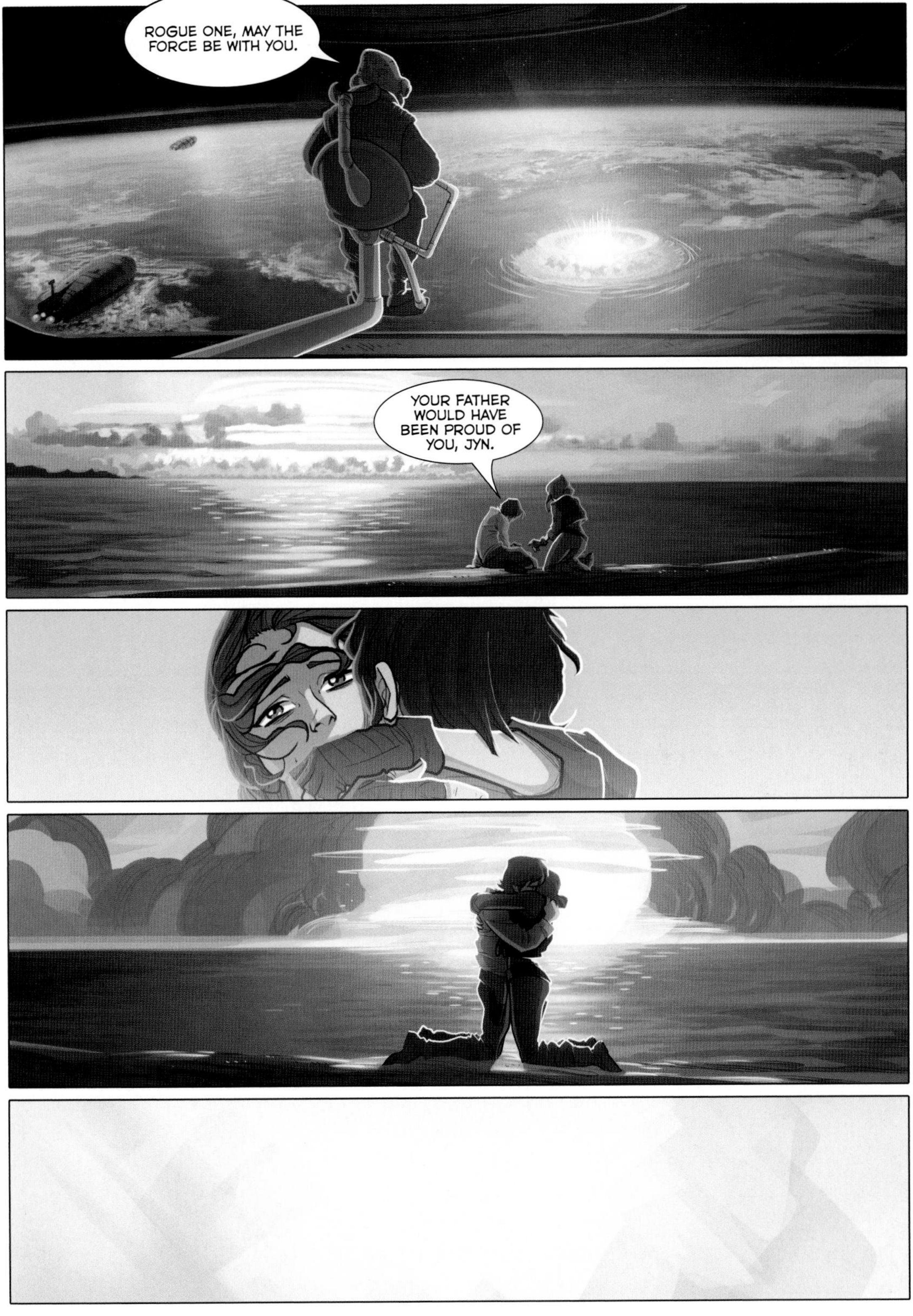
ROGUE ONE, MAY THE FORCE BE WITH YOU.
YOUR FATHER WOULD HAVE BEEN PROUD OF YOU, JYN.

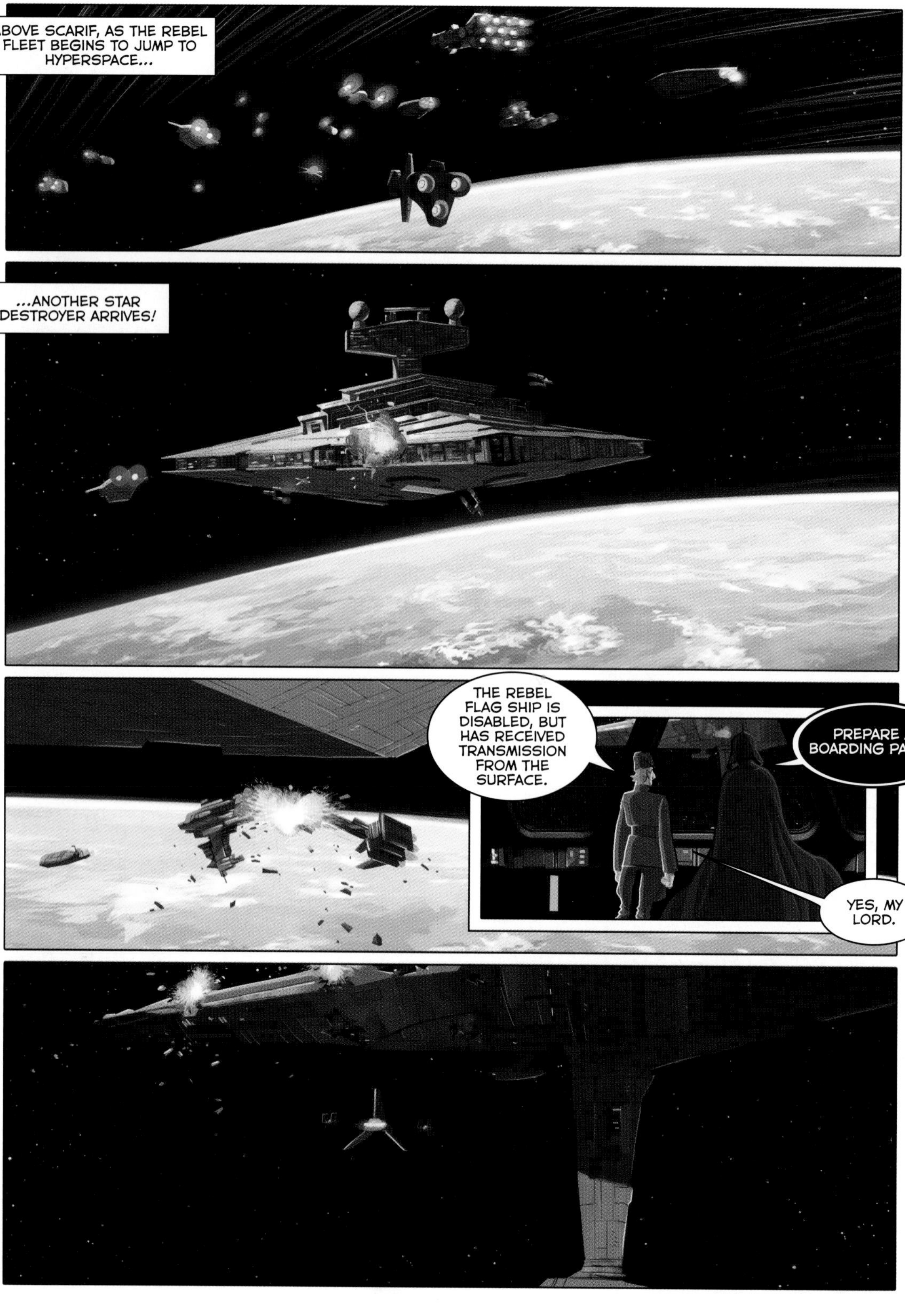
ABOVE SCARIF, AS THE REBEL FLEET BEGINS TO JUMP TO HYPERSPACE...
...ANOTHER STAR DESTROYER ARRIVES!
THE REBEL FLAG SHIP IS DISABLED, BUT HAS RECEIVED TRANSMISSION FROM THE SURFACE.
PREPARE A BOARDING PAR
YES, MY LORD.

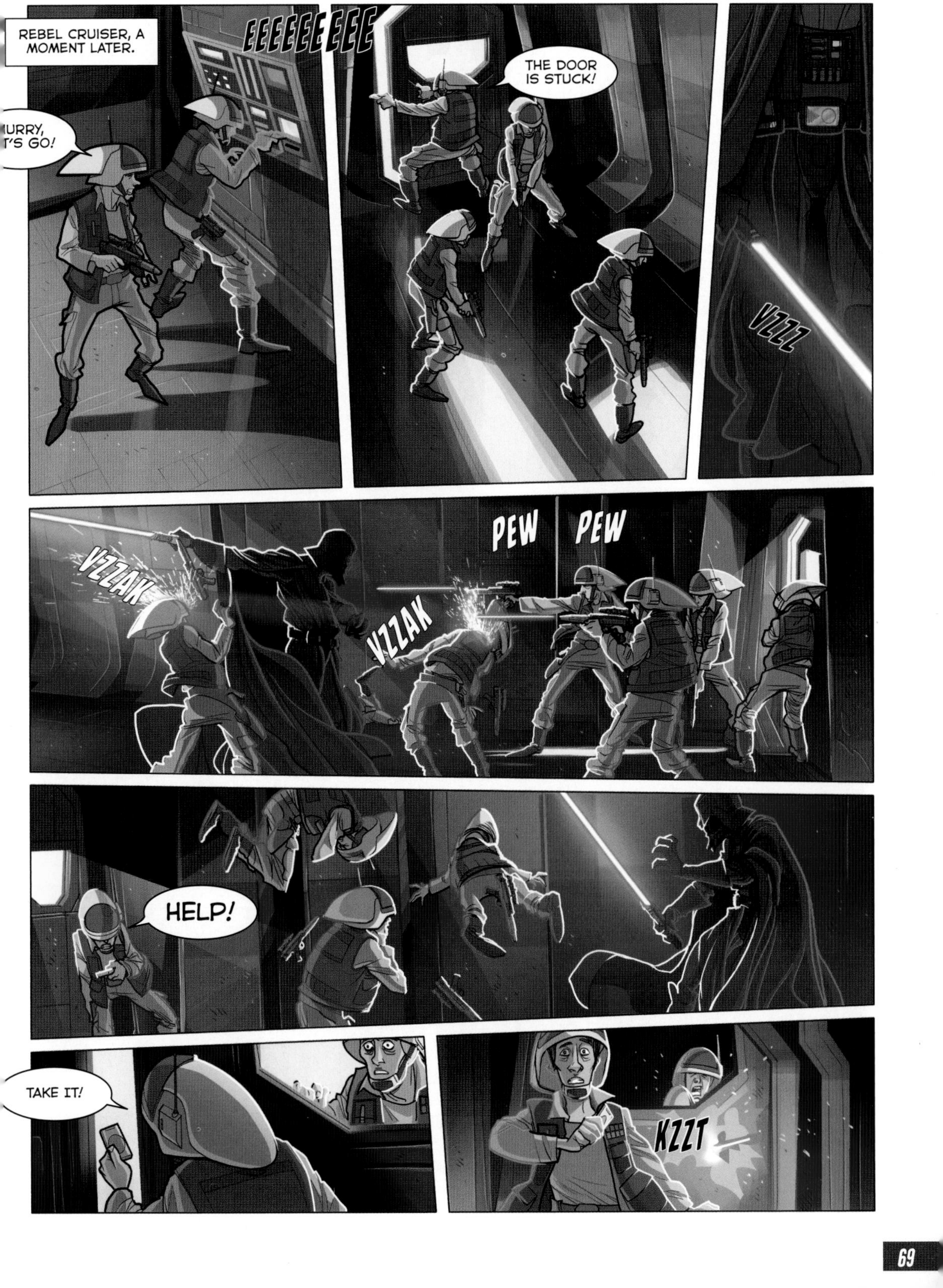

REBEL CRUISER, A MOMENT LATER.
EEEEEEEEEE
URRY, T'S GO!
THE DOOR IS STUCK!
VZZZ
VZZAK
PEW
PEW
VZZAK
HELP!
TAKE IT!
KZZT

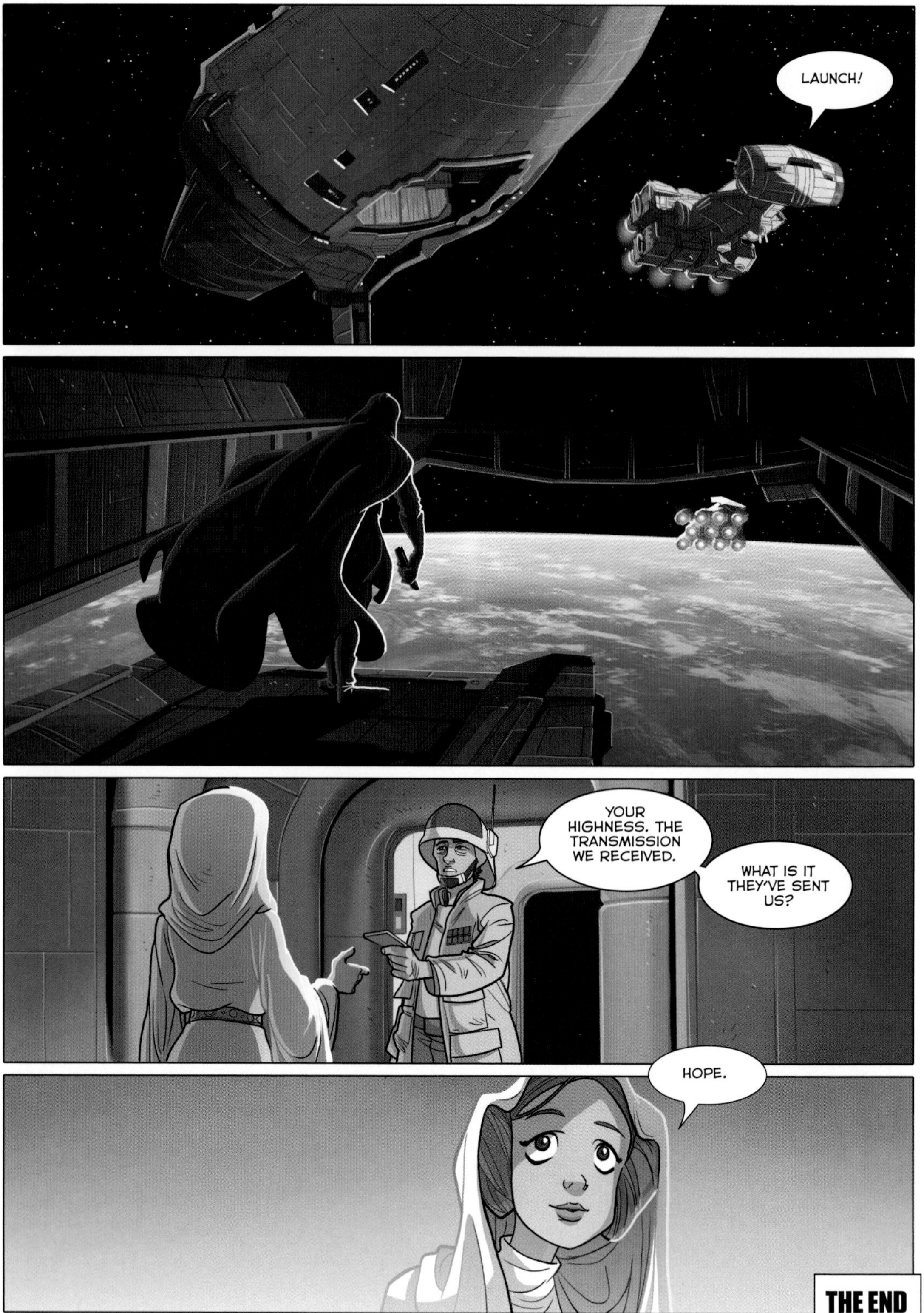
LAUNCH!
YOUR HIGHNESS. THE TRANSMISSION WE RECEIVED.
WHAT IS IT THEY'VE SENT US?
HOPE.
THE END

"YOU'RE NOT THE ONLY ONE WHO LOST EVERYTHING. SOME OF US JUST DECIDED TO DO SOMETHING ABOUT IT."

CASSIAN ANDOR TO JYN ERSO

CREDITS

DISNEY PUBLISHING WORLDWIDE

Global Magazines, Comics and Partworks

Publisher
Lynn Waggoner

Editorial Director
Bianca Coletti

Editorial Team
Guido Frazzini (Director, Comics),
Stefano Ambrosio (Executive Editor, New IP),
Carlotta Quattrocolo (Executive Editor, Franchise),
Camilla Vedove (Senior Manager, Editorial
Development),
Behnoosh Khalili (Senior Editor),
Julie Dorris (Senior Editor)

Design
Enrico Soave (Senior Designer)

Art
Ken Shue (VP, Global Art),
Roberto Santillo (Creative Director),
Marco Ghiglione (Creative Manager),
Manny Mederos (Creative Manager),
Stefano Attardi (Illustration Manager)

Portfolio Management
Olivia Ciancarelli (Director)

Business & Marketing
Mariantonietta Galla (Senior Manager, Franchise),
Virpi Korhonen (Editorial Manager)

© & TM 2017 LUCASFILM LTD.

Manuscript Adaptation
Alessandro Ferrari

Character Studies
Igor Chimisso

Layout
Matteo Piana

Clean Up and Ink
Igor Chimisso, Stefano Simeone

Paint (background and settings)
Davide Turotti

Paint (characters)
Kawaii Creative Studio

Cover
Eric Jones

Editors
Justin Eisinger & Alonzo Simon

Collection Design
Clyde Grapa

Publisher
Ted Adams

Special Thanks to
Michael Siglain, Frank Parisi,
James Waugh, Pablo Hidalgo,
Leland Chee, Matt Martin

Based on a story by John Knoll and Gary Whitta

Screenplay written by Chris Weitz and Tony Gilroy

For international rights, contact licensing@idwpublishing.com

ISBN: 978-1-68405-220-2

20 19 18 17   1 2 3 4

www.IDWPUBLISHING.com

Ted Adams, CEO & Publisher • Greg Goldstein, President & COO • Robbie Robbins, EVP/Sr. Graphic Artist • Chris Ryall, Chief Creative Officer • David Hedgecock, Editor-in-Chief • Laurie Windrow, Senior Vice President of Sales & Marketing • Matthew Ruzicka, CPA, Chief Financial Officer • Lorelei Bunjes, VP of Digital Services • Jerry Bennington, VP of New Product Development

Facebook: facebook.com/idwpublishing • Twitter: @idwpublishing • YouTube: youtube.com/idwpublishing
Tumblr: tumblr.idwpublishing.com • Instagram: instagram.com/idwpublishing